PRAISE for *An Am*

A transportive, deeply intellige
visionary gift.
— China Miéville.

A major arcana of death in America, shot through with bullets, black humour and an assassin-artist's eye for detail of place and thought. Kirsten Norrie has crafted an ocean-crossing, stricture-defying masterpiece: flamboyant, bloody, piercing, rapturous, brutal, unforgettable.

Everything here - embalmers' techniques, arcane conjurors' potions, the flora and fauna of the old West - feels drawn from the life: from 'freight carts stood like vertebrae' on a rough plain under the dawn, to its darkest scene, a prose Velázquez painting of a sabbat of Mexicana.

The many deaths in *An American Book of the Dead* are not trick-scares put there to punctuate the narrative. Mortality here is the centrepiece, death the dark polestar, the relentless attraction of the story: death of the body, of decency, of injustice, set amid the most exceptionally alive descriptions of the fleshy and psychic equipages of life… The taste of planets in snowflakes, the notion of a gap in time between life and death, of time thickening between two minds watching each other, of the tragedies of wolves and men. Stalked by the story of a scalping from the Kansas frontier and weaving her way to a riveting, layered conclusion, Norrie takes exhilarating risk with the novel form. Her characters speak in interruption of each other's thoughts, which are our thoughts, which are our dreams. This haunted troupe looks up at us: they live burningly towards us, out from this monumental, opulent book of the dead.
— Damian Le Bas

Norrie is a visionary writer, whose extraordinary first novel — *An American Book of the Dead* — draws the reader on an intrepid dance through human history, the dark subject-matter illuminated by an imagination ablaze. Haunted by the voices of Wild West ghosts who eat at your heart, mind and table, An American Book of the Dead drastically revivifies the Western in form and scope.
— Nancy Campbell

AN AMERICAN BOOK OF THE DEAD: A WILD WEST SÉANCE

Kirsten Norrie is a writer, artist and musician. Her work has appeared in the Guardian, the TLS, the Scotsman and on BBC Radio 3 Late Junction and the Verb. In 2024-5 she is the Judith E. Wilson Poetry Fellow at the University of Cambridge and was previously an AHRC Kluge Fellow at the Library of Congress and a 2019 recipient of a Fondation Jan Michalski writer residency in Switzerland. The MacGillivray archive is held at the Scottish Poetry Library. www.kirstennorrie.com

Also by Kirsten Norrie

Dream of the Cactus Garden   (Nightjar Press, 2024)

CONTENTS

ISBN: 978-1-916938-61-8

Cover designed by Aaron Kent

Edited by Cathleen Allyn Conway

Typeset by Aaron Kent

Broken Sleep Books Ltd
PO BOX 102
Llandysul
SA44 9BG

An American Book of the Dead

Kirsten Norrie

Broken Sleep Books

After the bones had been cleaned in the laboratory, it became apparent that the skeletons had commingled. While the bones were in storage at the community college, a number of boxed bones had been coalesced — how this happened, no one knows.

MICHAEL FINNEGAN, 1973 ARCHAEOLOGICAL
REPORT ON WALNUT CREEK MASSACRE, 1864

No sooner had our men surrendered, the rebels instantly commenced robbing the train, and murdering their prisoners, even the wounded. Here is the scene, or a sample of it, ten minutes after. Among the wounded officers in the ambulances, were one, a Lieutenant of regulars, and another of higher rank. These two were dragg'd out on the ground on their backs, and were now surrounded by the guerillas, a demonaic crowd, each member of which was stabbing them in different parts of their bodies. One of the officers had his feet pinned firmly to the ground by bayonets stuck through them and thrust into the ground. These two officers, as afterwards found on examination, had receiv'd about twenty such thrusts, some of them about the mouth, face, &c.

WALT WHITMAN, MEMORANDA DURING THE WAR

'I have,' said he, 'made the soul of a boy, unsullied and violently slain, and invoked by unutterable adjurations, to assist me; and by it all is done that I command.'

SIMON MAGUS, THE RECOGNITIONS OF CLEMENT

Death has indeed been here, and its traces are before us; but they are softened and deprived of their horror by our distance from the period when they have been first impressed. Those who sleep beneath are only connected with us by the reflection, that they have once been what we now are, and that, as their relics are now identified with their mother earth, ours shall, at some future period, undergo the same transformation.

WALTER SCOTT, OLD MORTALITY

Death is a mirror which reflects the vain gesticulations of the living.

OCTAVIO PAZ, THE LABYRINTH OF SOLITUDE

E. E. HENRY, Photographer.

ROBERT McGEE,

Scalped by Sioux Chief Little Turtle in 1864.

I

The Summoning

I

WILD WEST SÉANCE
LEAVENWORTH, 1890

A BAND OF THOUGHTFUL PEOPLE

"THE FIRST SPIRITUAL ORGAN-
IZATION OF LEAVENWORTH"
A BAND OF THOUGHTFUL PEOPLE

The Charter Which Was Paid For by
Small Contributions Has Arrived
From Washington — The Asso-
ciation Starts Out With
Ten Members — Mr.
E.E. Henry, an Old
Citizen, Is Pres-
Ident

ONLY ONCE IN A photographer's lifetime, comes an image which seeks its own revenge. Mine is seared into history's violence, scorched into myth and tired lies. And what would you say, were I to show you this image, believing it to be of some worth, thinking it conversant with the truth of another era's circumstance and so, indubitably, with your own — show you the uncrossed wires of magical transmission whereby the skulled flesh can be tinted in a salt and paper ground to defy the decaying brush of death itself, as if death existed solely within, already kept in the lungs, or the spleen, or the chest, perhaps to pump a ceasing, and then a slow self-carnage of stench and dissolution: that even that death-hearted, death-imaged and death-scented part would then rot and only the strident bones of admission could ever configure to let us know there had been — caged carefully within them — death itself, once living.

I am talking about the demise of a paper falsehood, of course — or rather, one that refuses to die. Recalling an errant carte-de-visite, one still displaying the blatant bones of its invention. That morbid photograph, housing its own virulent myth. . . if I could speak with it now, it would be to silence myself, but gone are those days of sittings and trance. You might say a photograph can't hold such power — but I should know, having conjured one myself: the impoverished magician whose camera lies broken, bust in the salts of the heart. Mine is a cautionary print, hot from the spirit rapper's table. A cautionary imprint of the studio set, played out in old themes of an American dead. It still calls to me now from dime theaters and sideshow tents as I see him emerge again and again, damaged and wilfully damaging. Did I summon him, or he summon me? Regret is such a strange offering, gifted to us by memory's contempt. My own regret has yielded futile attempts at revision: convolutions of a bloody history that vanish like acrid smoke to the touch. Now, there is nothing I can do to undermine this manifestation, except to try and overwrite his image in sign, scrawl and sleight of hand. . .

MID-LIFE I had taken my risk, relocated from Ontario to Kansas and found myself in Leavenworth, a wild dog and dust-board town razed by prairie heat in summer and suffering harsh winters. Stationed as it is — just a chipped stone's throw from the Missouri River — no. 322 Delaware Street becomes excessively humid in June and hard-bitten come December time. I might not have purchased the place, had I known the river's seasonal influence. My sitters departed, perishing, as the price of coal rose ever higher in winter. Summer proved worse: flies on the lens and sweating subjects.

Still, soon considered by some as Kansas' only photographer, I captured soldiers, murderers and immigrants; freedmen, militiamen and showmen; brides, nuns and spinster-teachers, come hell, hail or high-shine. Pictured Hickok in pellucid dark. Pictured Custer. Pictured William C. Cooke in his greasy sideburns. Pictured white families sweating in a seated pose at a table laid with old chenille and grimy paper roses. Black companions in a freezing set, picnicking on canvas grass. Here sat trail blazers, propagandists and tall-tale-tellers. I emblazoned their presences on salt-paper mirrors. A posed halomancy of the heart.

Gradually, I came to ply my trade on behalf of those indifferent to the Kansas weather, my meager income subsidized by the Leavenworth dead. Imaged old Mr. Montgomery, drowned at dawn in a disused well. Took the peeled-egg softness of infant Beth's skull, wan in a frill of christening robes. Photographed Laura Parmetar, a limp four-year-old dead from pneumonia. Caught Morpeth's hands, rigid as steel. Captured Mrs. Tudor Walker's fingers; each one blackened near the knuckle with the phantasmic stains of absent silver rings.

None so dead as the Kansas dead. Now unburnt by prairie days, those dead. Now untouched, those dead, by snow fallen. . . though a spring wind still sifts the bonfire's leaves, though scrolling smoke still winnows the ashes, hot, pink and tasty with fire. . . though a child of each descendant generation surveys another paper likeness, still nourished by death's own imprinted marrow.

Charged by a flash, I — as photographer — knew this.

Yet, lately — though society portraiture was my daily bread and post-mortem mementos watered my wine — I had developed a passion for the new photography and cartomantic occult happenings. For overlays, conjuration and depictions of the deceased as revived and shiversome presences. Had convoked a Band of Thoughtful People to summon up phantoms.

What a bad catalyst, rebellion. What a knotty contention with the father-desire, I — past thirty — still fueled, to impress he who frowned on the dead in spirit rations, who enjoyed my anxiety, my impudence, sought to put them both down hard. So craven and touched so, by obsession, I quietly kept house for the spirit world. My studio, become a Weather House of the quick and the dead, harbored the over-warm and the over-cold. Summer ushered in the living subjects, and with the bad light, winter drew in cadavers and wandering souls. No. 322 was a spirit barometer, I thought to myself, and took to putting a tin silhouette of a woman in the summer window and of a man in the autumn, each hung from catgut beneath the weatherbeaten studio sign that creaked in seasonal recognition of its own equinox guardian.

And so it seemed that finally the premises had come into their own as the inclemency of March slowly wore on. Between hymns and wraiths, this studio prop-box of winding-linen ectoplasm, underdeveloped spectral eclipses and glass-plate ghosts, still proved fascinating to me until, one night, a far stranger manifestation appeared: one caught on the mortal balance bar of time itself.

AT NINE that evening, emerging from the lonely darkroom, I rolled down worn shirt sleeves and carefully replaced my cracked wire spectacles. Taking a long drink of bronze water whilst surveying the empty yard, I heard Murthly's bitch bark into the cold night air. Dead maple leaves scattered in a light wind and then the breeze settled on a cloudy, dullish evening. I knew Tuesday night's 'Band of Thoughtful People' were now dispersed in that frozen darkness just like their own disbanded considerations. Done, was Macarius' necromantic skull laid bare on shifting Egyptian sand. Done, were libations of blood and milk. Done, the gold-cooking bum: the holy fool. Done, the medieval panther breathing in a tender dark, become the perfumed breath of Christ.

Yet, I was still undone by the damn letter and, retrieving it from a threadbare pocket, read aloud the scrawled verse:

'He no longer answers me, neither by prophets nor by dreams.'

Refilling my glass from the rusty faucet, 'nor by dreams,' I said to myself. My father, the Reverend Thomas Henry: he who would never be impressed —

Port Hope, 10th March, 1890

My Dear Son,

Your letter of the 12th of February containing a spirit picture, was duly received, I am now on my way to the. . . Biblical School, Standfordsville. . . And answer your letter by telling what I think of the spirit picture. . . I don't dispute but what the picture has been taken. It is not of God, in my humble opinion, But of the Divil, and shows very clearly to me a falling away from God, and disbelieving his word. I look upon modern spiritulism as a fulfilment of proffisy and their mediums as possessing familiar spirits who were called in the days of King Saul, witches and wizards, soothsayers. For a proof of this please turn to Samuel 28 Ch. 3rd. . . .

"I see a ghostly figure coming up out of the earth."

"What does he look like?" Saul asked.

"An old man wearing a robe is coming up," she said.

Then Saul knew it was Samuel, and he bowed down and prostrated himself with his face to the ground.

Samuel said to Saul, "Why have you disturbed me by bringing me up?"

"I am in great distress," Saul said. "The Philistines are fighting against me, and God has departed from me. He no longer answers me, either by prophets or by dreams. So I have called on you to tell me what to do."

Well, son, you might have taken the old prophet's picture, and now I would not wonder, but what Dr. Slaine and his medium might get a picture of some of your friends if so, do not send me one unless it proves my feeling on the matter useless.

Myself: Ebenezer, youngest of four —

You well know you have left me out in the cold, as it were, I had replied passionately to him, and I have had to paddle my own canoe for myself. You have as you say in your letter helped all the rest, but me, and now you tell me that I am the _favorite_. Well, God knows I am glad and hope it is so.

I wandered back into the parlor light and trimming the lamp wick, brought down the flame, cursing softly as I burnt my thumb.

'Ah well,' still wincing from the scorch, 'nothing quite like the father's approval.'

But perhaps childhood was when such cold had first set in and I came to know the winters as especially threatening. Fluids frozen in the pipes. Flues blocked by leaves or nests. Recalled my Ontario boyhood days, how the blade of Neighbor's ax had cut a sharp clang through the woods. Straight as a die. The weight of that blade alone, had clear-hewn the resting log.

'Mr. Bentley!' My tongue flaccid with cold as I crossed frosted grasses toward the rising line of thin blue smoke, I'd stood and waited as the woodman split another chip and bent forward, ratting it apart, waited to voice my urgent question.

'Mr. Bentley?'

'Yes —' the ax had cleaved his words in two '— Eb.' He paused, breathing out air like smoke.

'Can you tell me about the angels again?' I'd said, tearful with cold.

Neighbor then turned away from his weapon, placing one booted foot on the rotted stump, wiped his nose with the back of a glove and began to speak it out.

'Well, there were angels since the beginning of time, ones with frosted wings like yon leaves and ones with wings of flame, but others with no wings at all, those being the most scarce to find. All flew and none hid. And they had names, all the names of the world, like the languages they spoke. And some had tongues of flame, others of snakes, and were terrible and dangerous.'

'What did they look like?'

'Well,' Neighbor gestured, 'like the bonfire smoke there. See how it takes on the hue of its surroundings. Or, perhaps the atmosphere appeared to smolder as an angel passed —' he pointed to the heat-distorted air '— like that. Smoke-colored seraphs. So you see,' he added, reaching for the ax, 'they were a strange breed. Some time, when you come out here again, we might go about finding one. I hear they haunt the hickory patch.' The strike of his airborne blade produced another clean chip. 'Tell your pa he can have some of these here logs. I have no need for all.'

'Y'ssir.'

Old tricks had been learned from Neighbor when the wet-necked ponies strained to be fed at the pasture gate. Gingerbread mixed with frankincense squeezed under the armpit, then held downwind, would bring them all trotting in. If you gave them a bit, they stayed and nudged you with dark muzzles.

That was spring, when the mustang's coats were snow-whetted from storms that flushed the sky and dissolved into fresh-stalking sunlight again. That was months before the air grew thick with the heavy grief of the men; thick with dry crackles as their cold-roughened lips drew on tarnished stems of hand-rolled cigarettes.

Neighbor, Joseph Bentley's wake.

A table of headless bodies wreathed in smoke, their staunch hands tapped with emphasis on the wooden surface, tapped out the meaning and circumspection of their plans. Theirs were heavy, feeling digits, jammed up with the damp stems of those cigarettes. Though the notices were not yet made, all had come and sat for the man. Then had stood for his internment, hats to belts, chins to chests, and the parson said musty prayers that rose in motes to the hapless godhead atop a tree, looking askance at this broken land of enforced Eden and its degenerate wares.

Amen, had motioned the preacher. Finally, the coiled rope of death had won.

I knew it.

The mourners stumbled in the cold sunlight as they came away in ones, twos and threes, back to the pastures and cultivated fruit crops they called their own and the boarded church door whistled in the wind as the pastor departed, striding down the mud-clad road, his dust-black garments beating him along.

I'd jumped the icy creek then, wandered toward the center of the woods, to the barn haunted by greasy chicken skulls and split sacks of corn seed. A careless winter, Neighbor would have said, looking over the damage caused by rats.

What lacked carelessness were those — his paper snowflakes — precisely formed with steel scissors.

'They're like water flowers,' I'd once said, turning over a delicate cut-out. Bentley had unfolded the contents of his hoard on a black, velvet napkin laid out on his kneecap.

'Tis of interest you say that, Eben. Every snowflake has at its core not water, but a grain of dust. Oh, it can be anything.' Bentley settled back, large hands clasped in his lap. 'A grain of pollen, star dust, meteor matter. Tis grown, like the pearl, on grit. And do you know,' he closed his eyes, 'that you can taste the stars. Planets too. Mars has a more peculiar taste than all. It is dark and thick, like the air before a winter thunderstorm, with just a quarter ounce of lightning.'

REPLACING THE lamp's ball shade as the clock chimed the quarter-hour, for a moment my milky features hallucinated the mantel mirror. I chucked the dead matchstick in the parlor hearth and watched reflected snow fall in the looking glass. A moving lens of March.

For tonight's sitting there had only been the two: a duo materialized in the icy garden, crossing bright parlor light cast on the hard ground outside. Their cold-thickened tones hung in the bitter night sky. Montgomery Slaine and Tudor Walker: the one a physician, the other a teacher.

'But it cannot be said that the Mexican Day of the Dead and spiritist meetings are alike in motivation at all.' Tudor had spoken loudly as they crossed the threshold, throwing off their gloves and coats, hanging up their sodden hats, and generally advancing toward the inner warmth.

'Thank you, Eben,' said Montgomery, his expression ironic, kindly, as I offered him a seat by the fire.

'I would suggest that the Día de los Muertos,' continued Tudor, carefully lighting a cigarette, 'is a communication between living and dead as a kind of gathering of souls; perhaps to unwittingly worship a gap in time where such things are possible. In any case, these are familial events to love and honor the departed. The séance is entirely different in its motivations. It always demands something, requires more from its dead and does not petition the deceased with necessary offerings. It is very much a dubious exchange in that regard. What do you think, Eben?'

'I think, gentlemen, we might begin with a glass of port. I have a very fine *Burmester Reserva Novidade* I am willing to desecrate.'

We had settled into silent companionship with our refreshments for a moment before I commented: 'you were discussing libations.'

'Let us dry off a touch first, Eben,' replied Montgomery amiably, but there was a caution in his voice which I'd taken to mean there had already been words between my two guests and that Tudor was oblivious (as ever) to the full stature of their meaning. Too late: the bait was taken. Enthusiastic for the poet's mound, was Tudor; the incubation of dream on a hill or in a circle. Drawn to cross-roads and thresholds, the cave and the abandoned house. How beggars and the unwashed are better communicants — spirits disliking human cleanliness. Talked about there not being enough words for dust: how for his students he had invented *shriff* and *shill* and *hirsutal* dust. Here, Montgomery raised his eyebrows. 'A *shill* is a confidence trickster, Tudor, as well you know,' he said. 'You're going to have to get yourself another word there.'

'Yet *shill* seems appropriate then, doesn't it?' said the teacher. 'To throw dust in your eyes. You see,' he continued, 'it is almost as if the apparatus of the sitting, the séance, is so clumsy as to defy the spirits to come at all and then — when they do — those who don't believe can dismiss it, because in general they don't.'

'Now Tudor, that's not quite right. Let's take the altar of high Catholic ritual, for example,' I interrupted, 'or even portraiture. I think it is more about fixing things in. Who knows if the Holy Ghost resides in hardened paste and wine, but the enforcement of that presence seems to mean it can leak wildly into everything else. Like the fixity of a portrait photograph. Doesn't mean the sitter's there. Even when he's dead. The vivid thing always abides someplace else.'

'Just as well,' said Montgomery wryly, 'the stagecraft we have here is a pretty basic one.'

'But that's just it,' said Tudor. 'Much better to give it an unconvincing focus, then it can be written off altogether. Merely the contraptions of ritual. The staging of theatrical belief, as Eben says. The real stuff, the rogue stuff, is out there.'

Evening moved slow toward night. We tried not to push Tudor around too much. When Abigail failed to materialize — and this across the span of several months — the widower abandoned the idea she had a residual soul. Now Tudor felt (though no-one understood this yet, only remarked on a sudden change for the good in him) that his wife's spirit lived on in their only daughter.

Yet, tonight had been constrained somehow. Bound together in a premonition of uneasiness, we three withdrew for the sitting to the shabby photography set. Paper slips marked with the letters of the alphabet lay in a circle round an upturned tumbler. This crude device was the psychograph, but we trusted it more than a talking board — just an ordinary glass, put to ordinary use, being purged on the weekday, of extraordinary spirits.

Because it had been almost as usual: just another Tuesday. The usual places and usual questions. The others had been hesitant, though. Made queries that required only a one word answer, a binary yes or no. No familiar others. No mediumistic elements. The normal hymns performed, the tired harmonium pedaled. A sitting evolved unremarkably on its planchette of reluctant will. It had perhaps, I thought ungenerously, been rash to open the Burmester. Yet, there had been a significantly odd feeling among us, the Band, and the wine had seemed a touch medicinal.

Now it was done, the querents gone — themselves ghosts in the night's recollection. Alone, I wandered the empty studio, lit a candle stub and began to make a pile of the sitting's notes. The wind was soft and rough outside, sifting flakes in a choppy breeze; a cold snap for late spring. Most unusual, I reflected, pulling the white scraps of paper toward me. They rested in a mound, like a croupier's raking. Worthless scraps of information, I thought then not knowing the stakes were high in the spirit offing. I laid my fingers lightly on the glass, tilting it a little. Then, a temptation — a kinetic temptation — overcame me and abruptly I snuffed out the candle-flame. The room fell into a deeper darkness.

What to ask...

'Rap once,' I said out loud, 'in the affirmative, and twice in the negative.'

I let the glass alone and asked the ceiling whether my father would relent. Silence resounded. Undeterred, I sent up another question. Nothing. Then I asked if the spirits might manifest a real ghostly form for my next photograph. There was a lone, light, scraping sound.

I sat stock-still. *Branches on the scullery window pane*, I thought to myself. Only, it sounded closer. Now a pause. *Ask another question.*

'All right — who will you provide for my next spirit portrait, a man or a woman? One rap for man, two for woman.'

For a moment, nothing happened. Then, there was a loud and single blow, this time to the inner door. I rose abruptly, relit the candle and went over to the studio threshold.

'Slaine?'

My voice hung unanswered in the flickering darkness. I remained still, listening for a moment, before finally flinging the door wide open. Cold air vigorously filled the studio. To my astonishment, there in the gloom stood a small figure, fist half-raised to knock again. The being was gaunt and ragged. Smelled sweetish with filth. Gripping a dirty bundle, it surveyed me with pale eyes.

'I got a question, sir,' it said.

ONLY ONCE in that photographer's lifetime comes a subject so exacting that the instincts are irreversibly sharpened in a moment. Mine had been dulled by the worship of séance: I could only see him as a manifestation of the outside world, counter-summoned by the evening's disappointment. My sympathetic vagrant — I can still recall him now: his shabby, wool greatcoat peppered with snow, his badly-fitting Union Army forage cap. The freezing air that rose from his shivering body, breath beyond dew point clouding from his mouth. *Looks too young for a veteran*, I remember thinking, *though was possibly a bugle boy*. My trained eye saw it all, took it all in, as if in a flash pan. Curiosity overrode a certain revulsion. Still, I wondered to myself just how he'd got in.

'I got a question,' the man repeated hoarsely, shifting the weight of his greasy-looking pack.

Well, then I'd invited him in and he stepped across the threshold — stepped over that threshold, like a beast across a stream. It impacted me in a way I could not have known then, though I took a sharp intake of breath as he passed. The stench of the man was something wolfish, tobacco-skinned. Then I thought to rekindle the wick and remember this because, as I turned back to the room, I unexpectedly dropped the lit match. (Careless, is what my father would have said.)

The vagrant had removed his hat and around his head was wrapped a soiled bandaging of newspaper sheets. I could just decipher the gazette's date. Tufts of hair protruded from the sodden print, his bedraggled beard was all-over wetted with tiny crystals of melting snow and his strange eyes were dirt-radiant. He seemed cautious, tensed in silence. So, we stood for a moment watching the match slowly burn out, leave its dark brand of evidence on the studio floor. Then I crushed the matchstick underfoot and carefully ushered my querent into the empty set.

I took his things then, explaining how that evening's proceedings were already finished up. But I was keen and watched over him as a retainer watches over the dead, waiting patiently as he dropped his oily pack to the ground and slowly undid his heavy watch coat — like a child fumbling over every last button. Then I took the stinking stack and dumped it in a corner of the hall. Just as I did so, a scrap of paper fluttered to the floor. I discreetly picked it up and, on a whim, on an instinct, pocketed it.

Then I was back in the room and pleased he'd sat down.

'Now,' I'd said, drawing up a chair myself, 'what is it you've been meaning to ask?'

There was a pause, the wick-flame bowing and scraping in the glass, blooming large shadows for us.

When the stranger spoke it was haltingly, as if proper voice had not been given to this question before: 'Think I've come here for spirits?'

You can blow a voice like that as if glass through the air of a room to the point of shattering. His voice walked out on a temperature beleaguered and bleeding. Had a kind of swim to it, I felt. I heard a dark gloss in it. Oh, he had a meat spirit all right, I saw it. His meat aged, daunted and hollow-boned from progressing through the infinite fields of his own spirit. *The spirit is outwith and to move through it causes decay.* What kind of spirit billowed from this being's tongue: crenellate and back-blown? A weary, darkened thing this face, scored from years of pushing through his own spirit's presence.

Watching him now — never letting the man's eyes leave my own fixed sights — I reached into a frayed pocket, retrieved and replaced the glass tumbler deftly upturned on the scratched table surface, arranged signary glyphs in a sphere of scraps around it. Done. I flared and subdued the lamp flame. Then I clasped the man's raw-boned hands and although the stranger had at first flinched at my touch, he now allowed his cracked and calloused fingers to rest lightly in my own. That dirt-sweet stench of his gently filled the room in a necrotic flowering.

'Sing a hymn?' I'd said.

We began the twenty-third psalm, fluid and violate. Somewhere toward the second verse my sitter broke off, damage in the line and I held the tune to the end alone, my thin voice wavering.

'Now we go to the pointer. Rest the fingertips of both hands on it.'

The flurry of hands in the dark felt to me a damp deck of shuffled cards.

'Go easy now,' I said to him, 'just a light touch on it, there.'

Then I began the summoning.

'Will a spirit develop here tonight? I ask one to emerge and spell out its given name in this material atmosphere.'

Lightning-quick the milk glass moved:

M   .

(There was a red paper arrow glued to the glass rim like a devil's tongue.)

This tongue now shot across to: *C*.

North-west then, still: *G*.

(The drifter whined softly.)

It shunted again to: *E* — then: *E* — then stopped.

There was nothing beyond.

'Does anyone here have a question to put to this spirit body? Do we have a querent?'

The vagrant cleared his throat. 'Yes,' he said nervously, in breath rusted by human voice. There was a pause.

'Go on,' I urged in a whisper.

'Would you make me a picture. . . take my likeness? Were commended as Kansas' best photographer in — down at — the gazette.'

Where is Macarius' bleached skull now, Ebenezer Elijah Henry? Lying beneath a blanket of snow on those sifting desert sands? Proceed with care: lend your psychograph wily tenderness, some.

'You didn't come down here for the spirit sitting? The séance?' I got up to increase the oil flame.

He regarded me evenly. 'No, Mr. Henry. Though I have learned from it, some.'

I suppose he must have seen my expression. I relit a half-smoked cigar, offered him a fresh one. We sat smoking for a short while. Presently, gathering myself, I said that I would of course picture him, but that I was booked until the end of the month, and what my fee would be, and so on and so forth. A studio portrait, I presumed. He said he didn't have that kind of money. I replied, surveying him carefully, that this was unfortunate as I could see he would make a compelling subject. He said nothing. Smoke rose between us in proxy wraiths. I withstood the silence a little longer. Then, I suggested, might not an exchange be made? And I saw this not as a cunning gesture, but one which held equal promise for us both.

I have never bargained with the spirits as the stakes, but it seemed to me, that this stranger who'd emerged from the darkness might be persuaded to resume our spiritist sitting. In return, next day, I said I'd take his portrait for him. Something about his presence made me crave a strong apparition.

And so in dedicated silence we resumed, holding hands in the refreshed gloom as I sat with the stranger in our summoning and spoke out loudly into the empty room: 'Do we have a spirit here that wishes to speak with us? Come and show yourself, show yourself now to us. . .'

II

The Vision

An account of the séance witnessed by E.E. Henry
as summoned from events surrounding Robert McGee
through various, deceased spirit others
— 21st March, 1890

I

SÉANCE: E.E. HENRY PHOTOGRAPHIC STUDIO, LEAVENWORTH

Familiar spirit: Jerome Crowe, wagon master

'THEY SAY A SCALPING sounds like distant thunder, but no rumble troubled us that day, nor none beyond. The dawn was clear and the dawn was calm,' said a spirit figure, coming toward me. 'I'm Jerome Crowe, wagon master of this here freight train — how do.'

He had an easy, friendly manner about him and blue-astute eyes and a small frame — taut and lithe from long years droving and shinning around, I thought, but he was also tough-respectable looking and his coat was well darned.

On the rough track behind him freight carts stood like vertebrae in a straight-backed spine that led to a fort in the middle distance. There were thirty or so wagons hitched to six yoke of oxen apiece: a column of jute-covered Murphy wagons, soft in the half-light. And among those wagons stood sixty or so spirit men and boys: freighters, drovers, cattlemen. The air was starred by their cigarillos which glowed in a scarlet galaxy as the men smoked by mouth alone, their hands being full-occupied with reins and coffee tins, hard tack and bullets. All was quiet in the eastering, save the chafing of tackle and light nickering of ponies. Men and beasts in the company waited, as slowly the darkness dried up among them. And I watched those ghosts wreathed in cigar smoke, as the one who'd spoken to me outstretched his arm. I shook his hand and felt my nervous system recalibrate.

'I expired on this old trail around quarter past six on July 19th of 1864,' he said, mounting the box of a nearby wagon. 'Will show you how it happened. That youngster there went with me, asleep in the back on a sack of flour —' he gestured to the wagon rear, 'was hard to tell his age, so ruined by hunger. Come on up here, if you like, I'll show you the death trail in all its lights.'

I took him up on the offer, clambering onto the riding bench and glanced at the sleeping lad with his dry, straw-colored hair.

'Can't rightfully say, whether that's his true shade or the sun's doing. First time I saw him, he looked a ghost anyways. Eyes like dirty water,' said Crowe as he made a sign at Dock Brockman, whose harsh whistle moved us along.

WE CROSSED Leavenworth county and Johnson, Douglas and Shawnee counties on that sandy-soiled artery of commerce and stopped to water the mules in Franklin and then again in Brownsville and in Council City worked lift-jacks to raise and remove the wagon wheels, lubricated front axles with tar from tar buckets that hung from the rear axles, before the whole freight train rolled on again toward Allen in Breckenridge county where we watered and were cornfed again and went on to Council Grove in Morris county before reaching Diamond City, the last stopping point, where we tar-oiled the axles again. From Diamond City we moved beyond the Plum Buttes, past the whiskey ranch, toward the Dakota sandstone of Pawnee Rock, criss-crossed with ancient petroglyphs of those tribes who knew the crag in all its senses as a powerful charging point, and newer glyphs of those passers-by who merely scratched their names in stone as evidence they once existed.

Around that soft brown rock grew clusters of plum trees whose fruit flesh when ripe fed wolf and human both. Then we traversed the honey-green waters of Little Arkansas Creek and Cow Creek, before finally moving onward toward Walnut Creek. The prairie desert was high-voluptuous in shimmering, seasick buffalo grasses that caught and glimmered the light.

'This was H.C. Barrett's supply train; as contractor he leaned hard for a fast freight,' Crowe said, offering me a cigarette. 'Gave me three and a half weeks to make it down to Fort Union — should've been four — but he left the route choice up to me. Maps would've kept us right, but more dead-on were our older drovers used to getting gold, Mexican woolen blankets and coffee from Santa Fe, turning right back around with ribbons, washboards, soap and candles, you name it. They'd got sugar, whiskey, shoes and molasses, silver bullion in bars, tobacco and hardware, cider, cloth and cured meats. Brockman, Bird, Ab Gentry. All gone now.'

When we stopped to set camp, I surveyed these spirit-drovers, The rucks, humps and ruts of the road showed as much on their faces as on the well-worn trail, and their eyes held distance as their only pale and discerning coloration. Excepting Crowe. His own eyes that cornflower-blue and good at anticipating tears. He glanced down at the boy again, speaking to me in a whisper.

'Robert McGee. Signed up too young as an orphan. There are tears in him yet. You thirsty?' he asked the boy who, still half-asleep, now roused and sat up.

McGee nodded.

'Here then, have some of this. Mind now,' he said, 'go easy.' Crowe passed him the flask, then turned his attention to the reins, wiping a ghostly forehead of dust.

The train picked up a phantasmic head of cattle Johnson way, four hundred and fifty head of jostling phantom beef and their spirit young: looming, snorting and slow-shaking those massive skulls, though none so massy as the buffalo's, and the dust clouds that rose up around them seemed to warrant the torpid exodus of an old citadel. Flies too, swarmed the moving camp and deadlier: mosquitoes. The freight line rumbled on in the heat toward the rusty cloud line, but no sign of near or distant thunder came.

'Men die out here easier than you'd fathom,' said Crowe cheerfully. 'I met one last year got bit by a rabid wolf and expired. Typhoid'll get you, pneumonia, the blue death, pleurisy, all those ailments of breath. They have a full range of expirations out here, one time spoke to a soldier froze to death, another man I knew got into quicksand. Better'd be a summer-walker, even if you do have to mind them rattlers. I'll have that back now.'

Sullenly, the child returned Crowe his water flagon.

'What age did you say you got on you, anyhow? Barrett's been making up numbers again. Look at you.' To me he added, under his breath: 'Looks like a mongrel's corpse.'

Memory now flickered in young McGee who recounted to Jerome and me the fort that once squatted quiet in a fold of the Mississippi River, indolent in the rising heat. How he was taken through to a meeting by a whiskered man in a sagging uniform, then delivered by hand to another spirit with a scratching pen that carried on until the lad's legs had ached, carried on until he'd answered his age.

"Strip," then said Captain C. Human. The boy had peeled off layers of worn and dirty clothing. Then the gaze; the summation of damage. "Dress," the captain had said. He had a hardened face and mopped his grizzled brow with a damp cotton square, and had sighed as he sat down, and set down his pen, and said: "Don't lie to me, son. Got tired of fruit picking?"

"Never tried, sir."

"Well, in that case, I suggest you get to it. Plenty of fruit about this time of year. Not enough lads to do it. Only post you would have had is as bugle boy, drummer boy or flute boy and those posts are all brim-full," said the captain. "Anyhow, looks like your skin's gone for bone. Dismissed." Slatted sunlight had cut hard through the cracks in the barracks room shutters. The boy had left with a dry mouth.

'Ah well,' said Crowe, flicking the reins, 'you been a wild rover now.' And he whistled it drily in the heat.

When the wagons halted at ten, lizards crept up and clung statically to the inner linings of jute awning. Smoke from cookfires rose delicate blue in an atmosphere of rising cerulean. Crickets throbbed in the noonday heat and the spirits dozed and twitched and dreamt or sat lucid, smoking, or wandered down to the gulley stream to work out the dirt from their scalps with river-wet fingernails. High clouds held still, and the sun beat down indifferently upon us. Wildfires had swept the blue grama grasslands and those ambrosia fires fermented the heat, parched leaves from the wild cottonwood, elm and willow trees and brought drought and upon drought, dust storms. Cones of traveling dust columns seceded the horizon and vanished livestock. Dust as a black ash that months later blackened rain and finally snow, a snow suffused with a smokey taste. Black ash and sand ash and sere ash. All kinds of ash traversed the land. And the phantom prairie stock chuckled to itself as if a curse was upon us as we now harrowed our righteous trail without thinking warnings. Night pounced a trillion cinderous stars that whispered motes of light and when one morning the boy awoke, ash like snowfall had coated his sleeping form making him look an ancient figure emblazoned with volcanic spume. Ash fell on the horses, turned the beasts from dun to white, then piebald across the morning's light as the newly lifting breeze cleared patches from them, revealing their livery beneath. An ashy scum marbled our reveille coffee and I watched the boy, blear-eyed and ash-eyed, attempt to skim it off. Burnt fingers, burnt thumbs, were the only result as the ash spoke, whorled in the grain of a numinous language, speaking misfortune in the tongue of the land. None were sentient to its voice.

'Got some dirt in my coffee.' McGee whirled it about with a little stick.

'Won't hurt you none. It's merely minerals seasoned in the wind. We always called it prairie pepper. See any sign in that there cup, any omen?'

The boy peered into his cup. 'Nope,' he said. 'How long is this here trail, again?'

'Some eight hundred and thirty-four miles, Leavenworth to Santa Fe. Fort to fort. Approximate progress per day: sixteen miles.' Crowe tipped his dregs to the ground in a deft motion. 'C'mon,' he yawned, rising up off his haunches, 'they're starting to move on out. We'd best get set.'

Now that ghost trail was hard going. Four herders drove the cattle; two worked by day as the night herders bunked down and come evening, they swapped. Then the day herders slept, while the night herders kept guard over livestock corralled by those thirty wagons. At nightfall, the men tacked up makeshift tents. Before dayrise, took them down again. And they were up in moonlight and down in moonlight, for coolness and for quietude. We ate hardtack and salt beef and drank brackish water. Shaved in a bit of dancing mirror. Slept beneath the high-framed freight wagons. Midway across the Kansas prairie, I got to know others of Jerome's spirit companions. There was red-haired Boultby and Jan Grierson, then Perry and George, the two freedmen who stuck together and the Beabees — father and son. With them went boy drover, Allen Edwards — the one McGee signed up alongside. Lewis Sampson was close to Robert Lucas (as a youth on the farmstead, Lucas had been into mule-dudeism, getting the mule coats shaved just right, hanging fox brushes from their bridles. Out there on the plains, used coyote tails.) Then there was William Olohan (strong with a fiddle), and the morose James Kassel. Then William Redding, A.M. Gentry and Dock Brockman, the last three all of Brownsville, Nebraska. The last three: old trailsmen, old friends. All now dead.

ONE SABBATH day we paused for rest: 'As usual,' Crowe said and hunkered down near the horses, knuckled his mouth and gargoyled sound through a rusty harmonica.

'Metal's got grit in its teeth,' he grinned and ran a ragged arpeggio up and down the square holes. Crickets scored that midday heat.

'Here,' he said, 'off we go,' and lit up the scene with Yankee airs, Union airs and an old Spiritual. It was early yet, but the heat had grown intense, watchful. Crowe played 'Lorena' and 'Dixie' and 'Home Sweet Home' before there was hollering at the end of the line and presently the ghost of Brockman trotted down toward us.

'Been three or so riders at the herd,' Dock said to Jerome, not pausing to dismount.

Crowe got up then, squinting. 'Yep, I seen them right enough. Ok,' he said, 'let's drive them in and hitch up and roll out. Dock, you tell it to the rest of the chain as you pass on back.'

'Shall do.'

'And Dock,' Jerome peered at the horizon, 'keep steady, now this time.'

'Guess so.'

The drover moved off, cantering and calling right up towards the front, up the flank-length of the thirty-strong prairie fleet. The wagons lurched forward woodenly and at the rear, the herd nudged and jostled, harried by three drovers who hollered and yipped matter-of-factly, their spectral voices high and bright in the cloudless sky.

Then spirit riders came down the line, stark and gaunt. Shadow horses traveled up the canvas sides on stilt legs. Some fifty or so boys held those hot spirit mustangs still. Feathers dipped in the wind on their headgear and their hair was glossy with grease and cut short on the right-hand side above the ear and their arm and leg muscles glistened lean and transparent and their faces were plucked hairless. As they stood still so too, I thought, did time stand with them.

The spirit boys came nearer now and some rode flat, chest to horse mane, leaning forward to shake hands with the wary teamsters. The youths were armed with quivers of slight arrows and parfleche knapsacks and their horses' manes were ornamented with cowrie shells and leather tassels and there a spear and there a knife and Jerome looked upon them nervous-calm, rifle resting on his lap, relaxed-seeming but cradling one of the only two firearms possessed by the entire teamster company. He kept a light touch on it, waiting.

'Easy now,' he said, watching intently. 'Gently does it.'

And they were doing all right, the spirit men and mounted

boys, in this momentous and melancholy greeting until a hard knock: the crack-whip of a backfired revolver sounded. Recognition among them. The mustang of the boy nearest to the firearm gave a start and Crowe saw sudden slaughter-fear in the eyes of the nearest mounted youth as he shriek-yipped and rode in and touched and out again and the men roared and Dock dashed along the line, wielding a bullwhip, and I saw the ground become a dark ruby in places under the dull yell of the men.

Then there was a cry as two freemen on a nearby wagon were speared, each through the throat, and one lay curled and fetal as his blood escaped swiftly in a black-bright halo around his ghostly head. The blood pooled indifferently, taking his ebbing spirit with it, and the ghost ponies' hooves smeared that bright meat-spirit, trotted blood-marks across the light soil.

'Stay here,' Jerome said to me. 'Keep down. Hunker down with the boy near that wheel hub.'

'Don't leave,' said Robert — blanche-faced — but the ghost of the man had already gone, spirit rifle in hand.

Then the blood-hawks were upon them.

II

SÉANCE: E.E. HENRY PHOTOGRAPHIC STUDIO, LEAVENWORTH

Familiar spirit: H.H. Clarke, surgeon

WHAT COLD BELL RANG the spirits warm. Abandoned were the milk-glass and letter-board. Abandoned: the clasped hands. . . as now I lifted a small glass bell from the debris and shook from it a soft ringing like salt shaken or flour, rang out a summoning that quaked the spirit world, then replaced its trembling hollow on the table surface of quiet wood. There was silence for a while, but the bell had opened a scene ahead, one littered with ash, stones and dust. . .

'Do we have a spirit that wishes to speak to us?'

He sprawled on the ground, a brain-blasted animal.

Someone shouted: 'One, two, three.'

'Do we have a spirit here that wishes to speak to us?'

In the thickening heat, the boy became aware of his own voice and his arm rose up, hovering in his mind. Looked like a tree clean eaten away by bullets. Quivered in a bloody mirage and then crashed to his side again. The crickets gnawed on. There was a croaking. He opened a split eye and watched.

'*Wa'r*,' it spoke slowly, '*wa'r*.' The voice started to feel toward the light.

'Are you McGee?'

Prairie lizards crawled over the voice and small flies blurred in dark clouds over its wounds.

'Are you McGee? Do you wish to speak to us?'

A few thousand eras later, when the sun crooned in

glints of shattered glass, the boy got up and wandered out.

'That's it, we know you want to talk with us. Show us what happened, McGee. It's all right. Show us what happened.'

And he came to a watering place and intoned gently and the mud there flowed and reconfigured and mouthed back to him and then the salt plain and the sad plain darkened, and the fierce plain thundered where his sense ran away with him, stretched thin and pounded thinner. . .

'Show us what happened —'

WITHOUT WARNING, a shout: 'Let's try again, now: one two, three —'

The counted call produced — as if by conjuration — a young boy hoisted onto the studio table in front of us, hoisted and jostled and heaped from a stretcher stained with blood. My heart quaked hard — volatile, as the spirit turned his face and looked at me, hair wet with blood.

Then I saw him faint.

'Good,' said a man who looked like a surgeon, stepping into the sphere of the table. 'That'll put him from pain for a while.'

I looked over at the vagrant who sat motionless across from me, deep in concentration.

Craning my neck, I saw from the surgeon's fob watch that it was ten at night: dark and over-warm. Flies pinged the glass of four kerosene lamps that soundlessly flickered in the crude infirmary we were now within. Overheated, I removed my coat and surveyed the place. This was evidently a surgical theater and at its heart stood a stout and scarred operating table — my studio worktable, now given a different purpose. Where the studio fireplace should have been, a door stood open to an adjoining medical store, somewhat given over to grain sacks and tack, and in the bunkroom beyond was a makeshift ward. Through a conjoining open door, I could just make out three men and a juvenile camped down on cots. Their cries and shouts and coughing were subdued in the malty air, but the surgeon ignored them, focusing for the moment on his young charge.

'Division H will bivouac tonight,' the surgeon said, surveying me coolly. 'Bring me some water — quick. When the lad comes 'round, he'll call for it again.'

Dazed, I did as he asked. Returning with a glass and jug, I passed them over with that strange mix of courage and horror, keen to see what would materialize, and shuddered at the momentary touch of our fingertips: my warm moons to his cold ones. A collision of estranged anatomies.

'Spirit,' I said, 'who are you?'

Sweating slightly, he drained his glass and looked at me again: 'Put it this way, the Boston graduating class of 'seventy-four has not prepared me for this. Nor military surgery at Union camp Fort Ellsworth. Nor the labor wards of Virginia. I have five wounded brought in off the field — three men and two boys — and only one lad here to assist, almost entirely untrained. My name is Hulbert: Surgeon Clarke, to those present. Will have to work as I speak,' he said, 'should ye be keen to know more. I still use the old Quakerisms 'ye' and 'thy',' he added, 'always refused to give those up.'

He now inspected the fast-breathing boy arranged in front of him on the rough trestle table. 'Four of those brought in,' he said, examining the child's bruised arms, 'have sustained a range of damage from light to life-threatening; a hip wound, a scalp abrasion, cuts and grazes to hands and neck, one bullet badly embedded: twisted through the bone like a stubborn fossil. The boy laid out before us is different. Private Hanna? Bring those linens here,' he shouted and though he did not mean to be gruff, such was his voice of manifest feeling.

Another spirit stepped forward then, nodded at me and made for the store. I watched it move torpidly, as if wading waist-high through fast running water. Turning my attention back to the surgeon's phantom, I was astonished to see a tear roll down Clarke's unshaven cheek and land wetly on the boy's grazed wrist.

'Must get a hold of myself,' said the gnarled Quaker surgeon's ghost, though his brimming ducts would not defer filling and so he let his head fall back and made as if wearily wiping sweat from his brow with a pale forearm.

Then the spirit of Hanna returned and passed him the fresh dressings.

'It is a catastrophe of error,' murmured Clarke, as he pressed a corner of lint to his flooding eyes and poured himself a mug of dilute rye. 'Because I've heard that drinking water staunches tears,' he said to Hanna, his acting apparition of a nurse, who stood quiet now in that battened down, fix-me-up operating theater, stood patiently waiting. He was nervous and thin, with sun-haunted eyes. Then the lamps flickered rapidly and Clarke set his mug down: 'Who is this? Do we have a name for him?' He checked the boy's pulse points without looking up. 'Any means of identification?'

Hanna retrieved the orderly list for him.

'Read it me, lad — ye can read?' the surgeon enquired, listening to his patient's heartbeat.

Hanna flushed, began the names:

'July 19th

Deceased on the field, now buried at Walnut Creek: Jerome Crowe

Deceased on conveyance, awaiting fort burial: Robert Lucas —'

'Just the living, please.'

'Allen Edwards: A boy of ten or eleven,

James Brockman,

M. Gentry,

William Redding

Robert McGee of Coffey, Kansas: A boy of ten or eleven near

deceased on the field, won't survive —'

The surgeon interrupted again, 'this lad McGee?'

He gently drew back the boy's upper eyelids.

'Yes, sir. This here is McGee.'

'We are in perpetual need of light,' the surgeon murmured, peering at the boy's pupils. 'Shame it took them so long to get down there, could have done with the aid of an afternoon sun.' The old Quaker straightened up. 'And how old are ye, son?'

'Nineteen, sir.'

'This here thy first outposting?'

'Yes, sir.'

'Have ye seen much blood afore?'

'Not much.' Hanna replied, a little quickly.

'And ye, man?' The surgeon suddenly looked right at me.

Clearing my throat, I said: 'Not a great deal.'

'Well, mind me,' Clarke pointed to a small stool, 'if ye feel faint or feel ye may become stomach-sick, then ye go and sit there in the corner of the room til ye feel right again. It will come and it will go but ye can ride it, if ye catch it. We're going to be here until we've fixed these injured up. Bolt the door up behind ye. Bolt it there, Hanna.

Hanna shunted the bolt plank and then stood in attendance by the surgery table, awaiting orders. The surgeon tended intensive focus at his table and expected the young soldier-nurse to do the same, equipping him with concentration. I marked then how Clarke bore down on his young patient, a deciphering spirit, tools glinting in the hot-worked flesh.

The boy lay still on the operating table as they cut away his scant clothing. His ghostly form was naked and pale and glistened with sweat on that hot July evening, but he was still alive in the skin of the vision.

'This flayed area to the head is prolific,' Clarke said. 'We must concinnate this tender dermis, catch it before it turns necrotic. The flesh has been stripped near clean away from much of the bed bone. Seems what we have here is two blows and a partial evulsion. Yet — hold the lamp up please — perhaps it is a single evulsion raised on one side by swelling. Hanna, I'll take that blue stone water off ye now. This will likely granulate, and we may have to scrape it. He will be here with us some time if he fights and will need constant observation.'

Clarke surged a weak alcohol solution into the wounds as he spoke. 'Near catastrophic. I find astonishment in the fact that none of his major organs are pierced or grazed. No shattered flints, at least,' he said, outworking an obsidian arrowhead and another steel tip whose metal gleamed in the wicks' unsteady glow.

The kerosene lamps illuminated a sawdust-strewn floor which

now in-soaked blood, as the surgeon extracted bone-from-blood and blood-from-bone in this nerve-trying slaughter pen. Clarke put twenty-four stitches in McGee's leg and arm wounds, having prised out a broken arrow shaft, and his side was stitched up, and his groin, and an area near his left-flanking ribcage.

The boy sweated in and out of awareness and his pain was tremendous and at times they gave him a bite stick and at others, rye and Hanna held a water-soaked sponge to his parched lips and squeezed it lightly, spasmodically, watering him as if a thirsty flower. The young volunteer looked afraid of the screaming, but did not flinch as the surgeon worked tirelessly, provoking hot, dry shouts from the skinned boy's throat.

'Ye asked me who I am?' The Quaker surgeon addressed me again whilst quickly working over the last of the boy's abrasions and I leaned in to listen.

'It was not in this ill-equipped mud and plank theater, that I truly earned my M.D. stripes. A blood buster and siphon of cankers, I was no worse — no better — than any other Union army surgeon, only I wasn't yet a sot and had read the recent Nightingale report and heard of Lister's carbolic acid and rubbed my hands in a weak alcohol solution and washed my instruments the same, whereby men came to die less under me. Irony is, I died myself from poisoning of the blood. Where are we now?'

'1890,' I said.

He fixed me with a penetrating look and for a moment I forgot he was only a ghost: 'Ah, yes,' he said. 'Passed in 1889. Would have liked to have made a clear decade. Well, a cook would not work with fetid blood. Nor will I. Clean hands, clean heart, is my maxim. I specialised in cautery.'

All the while, the surgeon extracted stony fragments and

grit from the boy's limbs with army supply tweezers, disposing them in a tin bowl. He wore a large, leather butcher's apron. Kept scalpels in its pouches and a bunch of clean muslin pieces tucked in at its waistband and had tightly rolled his shirtsleeves high above forearms now cuffed in blood — but not his fists — in opposition to the usual red-handed surgeon, as he regularly sluiced both hands in spirits solution.

'Writing slows the mind's blood pace and cutting speeds it up. No matter how careful, ye are always racing the mind's blood and where that flows, follows spirit also.' He continued, almost under his breath now: 'what once had prevented me — a perverse spirit? — from rescuing the bizarre circumstance in which I had met a fatal case on the battered Chancellorsville field? A young soldier, suffering from typhoid fever with a bullet-blasted gut and a series of scorch marks on his brow near the blonde hairline? How could I have worked any the more skillfully then, knowing that in the dying face of that battle-whipped boy, lay the sudden features of my own son? Because death is a circumstance,' he mulled, now speaking as if to himself, 'which cannot be rescued by bringing other circumstances to bear upon it — *Jonah*. . . they told me I exhaled the name of my boy, slowly at night. He became my outward breath — *Jonah*. . . Since then: mark my drinking. I have a tremor in my left hand, both eyes constantly water. Was then discharged to Fort Larned, part-retirement, part-warning. They told me: nothing happens in a remote volunteer prairie outpost save the dust, save the wind, save the sun.' He paused and transferred the last of what he was doing to a small bright metal platter, adding sanguinary clots to make a full moon of bloodied silver.

Then he wiped his hands, crossed the room and walked

clean through the studio wall. Cautiously, I got up — fully risking breaking the trance. To my amazement the spectral lay-out of the fort theater enabled me to follow the surgeon's ghost. Where a door was superimposed (I could see the tired-looking wallpaper beneath the rough sod-work of the fort's adobe walls) I was able to move through it freely.

In the bunkhouse, I watched the surgeon at work on the three other damaged men. He fixed up a broken hip, retrieved a stymied bullet (close to lung), swabbed and stitched a ragged flank wound, cleaned and sealed a cranial gash and extracted an embedded arrowhead. Though the next day in their world had already turned, he finally attended to the younger child.

'That young Edwards lad,' he said to Hanna when done, 'has something of a head wound. Not so severe — a bullet graze, or perhaps he sustained a blow to the cranium. He is too fatigued to talk at present, but at some point we shall find it out.'

Morning crept further toward first light. Clarke returned to McGee to administer water and found him still living in the stitch-work of his mutilations.

'Because shock alone will age a being,' said Clarke to me, 'even unto death itself.'

Then he downed his immaterial tools, cleaned his phantasmic hands again and roughly commanded that Hanna keep ward watch. Before the ruddy thews of the muscular dawn, it seemed the old field surgeon had found his own exhaustion; beat a retreat to the medical store and slept there a full two hours. (For even spirits sleep, it seems, and I was still learning their incongruous ways.) As it was, his slumber helped matters like air poured on a fiery grass.

III

SÉANCE: E.E. HENRY PHOTOGRAPHIC STUDIO, LEAVENWORTH

Familiar spirits: Rebekah Crowe, teacher & Ruth Crowe, daughter of Rebekah and Jerome

'THIS IS THE SPIRIT of Rebekah Crowe, wife of Jerome, and I am here with the ghost of my daughter, Ruth.'

She spoke as if down a telephone, as if predicting the wire-line and voice piece of near-future communication, as if uttering that next era in. Her ghost now crossed swiftly to the studio window whose shutters seemed newly transparent as daylight flooded my photography set. The air was a pale topaz, as if the crystal's color had been diluted or bled, as if the gem's blood had gone bad.

Carefully she put her spectacles on, hooking a metal arm over each ear, and shuffled the letters delivered that morning.

'Saints alive, it's a wonder you can see anything at all,' she self-admonished. 'Not my fault, was born near-sighted. Never saw who was looking at me. Never saw fit to peer at them back. Thought the world a greasy one.'

Now she took her seat in the rocker and let three letters slide into her lap in favor of a small packet, turning it in her capable hands like a parcel of coffee or dried flowers, like a bundle of something deep-wise contained, precious, but yet needing prised apart. 'Jerome gave me that letter-opener last Christmas,' she murmured, then called out: 'Ruth!'

Silence thickened the rising dust motes, then a distant response sounded three syllables.

'Yes, mama?' said Ruth, sudden in the door frame. She had

raced through no. 322. Delaware Street — her bursting breath now spoke it out.

'Helter-skelter skeleton,' her mother said. 'Ruthie, fetch me the letter opener, would you?'

'Yes, mama.' And Ruth was off again, a spirit clattering the floorboards. I heard her rummaging in the rooms above. She returned in triumph, the unsheathed weapon held aloft: faux-dagger, faux-knifeman.

'Stop that now,' said her mother, looking up. 'Here, give it to me. It might be blunt, but it still has precision.'

Ruth, all glamor, dropped the letter-opener softly into her mother's lap and settled down under the window.

'Last year,' Rebekah said to me, 'my husband had glass panes put in and now the wind seems to howl a full octave lower.' She turned her attention to the packet. 'Have you your sewing?' she asked the girl distractedly, not looking up.

'In the other apron.'

'All right, then. Want to hear a letter from your father?'

The girl's spirit brightened.

Rebekah turned the package. I could see it was scuffed, its address inked, the corners damaged and the smudged seal loose a little. She slit the string and brown paper. Within were two missives and a thin jotter. Turning the jotter's pages she was challenged by a stuck part. She tore it a little, seeming to note the brown stain.

An ink blot, I assumed, but in thinking that recalled Jerome mentioned to me he hadn't taken his pen and this first page proved it, scrawled lightly in lead.

Putting the jotter aside, Rebekah instead chose a letter, smoothing out its creased pages.

Ruth looked on expectantly.

'Dear Wife, Family and Friends — dear sakes,' murmured Rebekah, 'can he never be the one to just address me? Must we have all else included in kind association? It's not as if they were in any proximity to hear him —'

'Why does he always write to *everyone?*' Ruth asked, listlessly.

Rebekah seemed disarmed and irritated by her daughter's more forthright questioning. 'Just because he does, dear. Doesn't want to leave anyone out.'

'He left me out — I am 'family', not Ruth, not Ruthie, or even daughter. He left me out.'

'Yes, he did and I shall remark upon that when he returns,' said Rebekah, protectively. She continued in a louder voice: 'Through the mercies of kind providence alone I am permitted to pencil this sad intelligence to you all. 'Pencil' being the operative word,' she murmured, but seemed unsure now, how to go on.

I sensed her swither — perhaps a vetting? Yes.

'Ruth,' she said, 'I need the bible to lay this out on.'

'But mother. . .'

'Now, don't disobey me, Ruth. Do as I say, there's a good girl.'

The young spirit called Ruth dragged a thousand limbs behind her, on fire with resentment like an ancient, manifold being whose flame-eyes gleamed. Young orchard-eater. She felt placed there for eternity and her mother only for moments and those moments were always filled with wanting.

Rebekah knew. Sensed her daughter's shadow again leave the room.

Now came her thoughts, intervening with my own, and for the first time in the whole sitting, I grew afraid of the ghosts.

'The day is full of its own hot sounds, heavy and lingering. I never

can take boisterous noise when like this. Am relieved the men are gone. Am clumsy too, which Ruth can't yet know; how the center of balance shifts. How everything becomes a quivering storm glass. And every month differs slightly. Every month's different. But some good comes of it — surely? You're more sensitive to the girls. You're a better lover to Jerome. When you start to paint again, that'll come better. And you know your lunar cycles, where it falls on or between moons.' Distractedly, her large hands smoothed the letter paper. ' *"This sad intelligence. . ."* well, perhaps a tacksman has died,' she thought, *'let us begin again with the journal.'*

Satisfied, she waited as Ruth returned.

'Will this do, mama?' Ruth's copper-brown plaits looked like thin frayed rope.

'We must get some vinegar for your hair, Ruthie. Where is your sister?' she said, counting the journal pages.

'Cutting things out. I brought my sampler to show you.' Ruth sighed. She slid down beneath the window again and threaded a darning needle:

 Here is the church and here is the steple.

A B C D E F G

There is June. There is mother. There is father.

(He is half done. There is no dog. The house is not there.)

Ruth Crowe, born December 1853.
 Her work completed on ~

'Better make it Christmas, Ruthie, you'll have it done for then. That needle's too large, you only need the small one for your sampler. Remember I showed you. That's it. Now there's a good girl, sit still while I read to you:

My Dearest Rebekah,

I am addressing this journal to you, not in case anything should happen to me, but because it always seemed a little strange to keep a journal for myself; the only person to have been and done and seen the events recorded. Anyhow it gives me comfort to have your listening ear, if only in my heart's old imagination.

<u>10th July</u> We started out a week and a half ago, as you know. I've been told this is the last job guiding. On Thursday July 1st we were done, loaded up by four am. Barrett had two young recruits with him, signed up late the night before. Came in together, I'm told, after failing an army physical. One is called Allen Edwards, but as they were separated, I was joined by the other strange sprite for this leg of the ride. His name is Robert McGee. His hair and his skin seem almost the exact same color. Pale skin, pale hair and pale eyes. I know Barrett has his schedule and his requirements, but this one does look awful young and if so young, not much use to us. Anyhoo, is better that he rides along than gets himself signed up. We lost enough boys on those battlefields to last God's lifetime. It's fair weather out here, R. Sun is high and hot, right enough, but there are still dew drops in the grasses come mid-morning. Dock's here again (I'm glad of that) and John Hiles, so we have got with us some good men for this leg. It will make things all the easier.

<u>11th July</u> Dock came down to see me this morning, said there's a rumor of more trouble on the trail. I asked him what. He says there was a scout passed through in the early hours, Brock had a talk with him, and says word

is the volunteer scouting parties are out. We should keep an eye out too. It don't console me to know I have one of the only two weapons. Leastways, I could head something off if it came upon us. There was a ring of wolves this night, but the campfires kept them off plus the three old work dogs we have here, tethered to the train head. In any case, come nightfall, we have the wagons corralled. Grub's not bad, I have to report, but if we had spare munitions, I'd happily spend a bullet or two on a roving rabbit.

12th July Weather still reads hot and fair. Nothing much breaks the horizon. The boy likes my harmonica playing so oftentimes I hand him the reins for a while and give him a few numbers. Hymns won't hurt him, but he doesn't seem to go in for those. Can't hold a tune, it seems. He don't speak much. He's pretty twitchy. We had beans for supper this evening, hardtack and jerky. Like I said, not bad going. Sunset would've clean taken your breath away and I do wish you were here to see it. If anyone could appreciate it, it'd be you.

13th July Hot and dull. Flies bad today. Not much to report.

14th July After yesterday's miserable entry, <u>something good:</u>'

These were the two pages stuck together in a brown stain. *Molasses*, Rebekah thought, *I can't prise them apart*. The bright blade of the letter opener flashed in her fingers, danced a reflection on her daughter's forehead. She noted Ruth was pursed with concentration at her sewing.

'16th July It transpires Barrett was aware of the increasing troubles en route. Should have better equipped us with weapons. We passed a train that even had an armed guard. Two rifles, Rebekah, is all we have and a limited amount of ammunition. Brockman pulled me aside today. He is full of dark mutterings. Feels Barrett is up to something. Why send us out on a troubled line when we could have waited a week or so. Thinks it has something to do with an insurance claim. I pressed him further, but he caught the boy listening in so we postponed our discussion 'til later. Drove the cattle hard today.

17th July Nothing as yet seen or heard of. Took to wishing I didn't know of any troubles, makes me nervy. Short with the boy. Then realizing I had to know, need to think on alertness, how to plan it out, suggested to Dock we travel together — he has the other gun. Dock said no, best keep one firearm up front with him and the other on me, down at the back. So now we've taken up the rear and are the last wagon. You should see the outline of Pawnee Rock.

18th July The boy frighted me today. We rested up for the sabbath. Come midday I sent him up front for some more hard tack. He came back along the line, but he seemed to me insensible as he got closer. His eyes where whited and he was still walking but he didn't answer when I called his name. When he came up to the wagon bench, I dropped down to meet him and saw his eyelids fluttering. Then he fell into my arms. Later, when I asked him, he said he got 'funny turns'. I think he's sick, Rebekah. I'm going to make him rest up in the back from here on. Keep an eye on him. We holed up all afternoon. It was fierce hot. A good, full moon tonight.

19th July Started early, a hard, hot sun, red in the mist this dawn. Not seen anything like it for some years. A beauty to behold. Morning's come in quick. Played harmonica for the men at lunchtime yesterday but I need to get myself some new airs. Have decided to work on some of my own across each day. Jerome's Jig, is the one for today.'

There was a large gap and Rebekah said softly: 'There's an entry missing.' She turned the page and found more entries congealed. Then, ushering me closer, read on to herself for a while, a chartomancy quiet and unknowing. I stood behind her rocking chair which creaked slightly, without real movement, and read over her shoulder:

'I returned and the oxen had bolted. At first, I thought the boy was trammeled by a great wheel. . . the wagon stood a little way off, but the oxen were gone, run off. He was lying face down, and I saw a large portion of his head skin had been removed, was clean off. Was near the size of a dinner plate. . . He's sustained some other harms too. I was loathe to move him, so I just whispered to him, got down on my knees. That's when the bullet got me.

Most of the men have departed: fled, or waited awhile and then made their way up to Fort Zarah. First part of the train took off when we were first hit. Poor old (or lucky old John Hiles) came back after tracking down a stray ox. He helped the others bury ten souls together (excepting the freemen who they buried apart) and though he wanted to stay, I insisted he get us help. He is sore worried the assailants will return. I said it is a risk we should have to take, knowing our ammunition all spent in any case. He has made me as comfortable as possible and seven others of us along with the boy who is in a sorry way. Last thing I recall was the whites of his eyes and foamy lips. He'd wet himself too, Rebekah, and his swollen tongue hung from his mouth like a dog's. That's when I knew he was done for.

I don't know any of us is long for this world. When this reaches you, I might be gone but these words still living. I hope they will reach you. It is thought, had a rescue party reached us by mid-afternoon, then I would have had a slight chance. Now, knowing the impossibility of this, I must tell you of my greatest affection for you and the girls. That they will grow tall and strong. Tell Ruthie and June I love them both. I would ask you to look the letter over and if you are satisfied, to take it down to the offices of the Nebraska Advertiser as soon as it reaches you. It has been dictated to Dock

Brockman on the understanding that it is purely for publication and will clarify details of these events. I must rest now.

Your ever faithfully loving husband,

Jerome.'

Rebekah Crowe winced in that strong beam of unreal sunlight, cramping in sudden pain. Ruth stood up then and surveyed me carefully.

'See what has become of us,' she said, the breeze from an open door lifting her tattered hair. 'Father is dead — you spoke with him. Shortly after, mother died from a womb bleed, the doctor said. I stopped eating, then and passed in 1866. We are stuck in this room, trapped and waiting. We read this letter every day at the same time. You came and mother thought we were released, but I think now we will stay here forever. Dusty, old dead birds. She'll be all right and I have my sewing. I have my sewing, Mr. Henry.'

Though Ruth was expressionless as she spoke, I saw tears course down the inner lining of her face, past the orbital bones and nasal cartilage, down her esophagus and into the close temperatures of the atrium and ventricle chambers, to flood out her small, pellucid and still-listening young heart.

IV

SÉANCE: E.E. HENRY PHOTOGRAPHIC STUDIO, LEAVENWORTH

Familiar spirits: George Bent, soldier & interpreter, H.H. Clarke, surgeon

AN EMANATION NOW ENTERED the room — not unblind to plagiarizing mirrors or glass, whose cold surfaces would recognize in passing this cross-wise energy of motion mostly ushered toward something called 'ghost' — one which seemed sensorily aware of its own condition which was the seed of the apparition's knowing and which, outlying, shaped its future intent. It was a copy of the shape of a life once extant in flesh. It was a male-scented, male-tinted ghost. This spectral man had come and stood awhile, unassuming. He turned a felt hat slowly in his hands like a soft wheel turning, round and round. Around that clock, the soft light glowed. Then he cleared his throat and made a beginning:

'When my father blew up his fort one dry fall of eighteen-fifty-two, saw how its dust burst pale across the ground, he must have known that this well-built adobe structure was an ideal army blueprint. He'd galloped back one dawn to detonate the newly deserted building. Left his family waiting at Short-Timber Creek. Rooks rose from the pines as his wife felt the displosion ripple through the morning half-light. Owl Woman saw that distant dust-cloud billow like smoke — loosened her careful grip on the reins. It was done. Gone was this great meeting place. The government offer of twelve thousand dollars had proved too untempting a price. My father preferred to quit the fort, leaving nothing much behind. Too bad. Those finely constructed adobe walls were the craftsmanship of Mexican laborers who had built them up using centuries-old knowledge of brickwork, warm in winter and in summer cool. Rain had patted down those clay walls and the sun baked them hard and smooth. Father broke and trained mustangs out there, traded in buffalo robes. Some years the Cheyenne wintered at the fort, making camp outside the walls. Some summers, before the war parties rallied, groups of Cheyennes and Arapahos sat talking and smoking clay pipes with white ranchers and Mexican drovers in Fort Bent's courtyard confluence, and travelers passing through oftentimes rested a month.

Fort Larned is different. Badly built walls allow in the rain, wasting encampment stockpiles. Storehouses are sunk in dilapidation, rainwater spoiling flour, beans, corn, and grain. The quartermaster has estimated well over five-thousand dollars' worth of animal feed has been destroyed this previous winter alone. Destroyed are those harder-ration food supplies destined for the Kiowa tribe camped in Fort Larned's shadow. Look at the state of it here —' and the ghost of William Bent pulled a campaign desk away from the wall, revealing corrosion and stains from rainwater that ate away at its rotted base. 'Dappled as a piebald pony flank. It's dry to the bone now, but come autumn it'll turn again. Whole fort's a pile of mush.' He shunted the davenport back in position. 'The men stationed here would be better building up these stone walls instead of going on useless buffalo hunts — the breastwork stands at less than two feet. What kind of a wall is that? They might as well be bivouacked. Fort's captain — a gambler and a drunk — can't size up the difference between starvation and defense. No man is in a good place here, not his people, not our people. My father suggested this garrison. He wouldn't now consider it worth the fuse. His own fort — Fort Bent — would have put this place to shame. Now it lies sifted on the wind, pulverized to fine New Mexico dust.'

I asked the spirit who he was.

'My name is George Bent: son of Owl Woman, son of Colonel William. My grandfather kept the Cheyenne Medicine Arrows. I speak in several languages, have been a Confederate soldier, was contracted as an interpreter. As a result of all this, I pass between worlds: I am not yet dead, but you see me in a spirit picture. Shall we go ahead and wake him?'

Now the surgeon materialized, half-asleep in heavy shadow. George made the sound of drumming rain with his left-hand fingertips on the table surface and I watched the surgeon emerge from his dream.

'Here,' said George and placed a paper by his elbow. 'That copy of the advertiser you wanted. Father said I should ride on over to you with a friendly warning. He cannot come himself, being tied up with the ranch. Asked me to stop by and bring you news — says you'll need morphine and strychnine supplies with what's brewing up. I'm on my way up to my mother's people. Don't want any trouble. Came to say also the mail line's down. You got any letters; I can take them and pass them along. Got a man on it who knows what he's doing. Been acting as runner all week.'

Clarke thanked him. 'That's kind of your father,' he said, 'send him my regards.'

'You're shaking.'

'I know it. Tis merely fatigue.' The surgeon licked his forefinger and thumb and spread the Nebraska Advertiser out flat on the makeshift desk. 'Let's see what this paper has to say for itself.'

I moved closer to get a look at the headline and became conscious of the close air in the timber-walled room, of physical scents on Clarke — as if he conducted a love affair with death who left light stenches of sweat and bloody mucus and black phlegm from the stinking, opened meat of bodies swabbed in spirits. The surgeon's snowy hair clung to his skull in stiff, combed furrows of grease and I thought it was curious that a man of such hygiene when it came to his patients, did not more carefully attend to his own.

'Ye are observing my hairline or the lack of it or the state of it,' Clarke said out loud, still reading.

'Yes,' Bent said.

'How I can let it get into such a state.'

'Yes.'

'What ye think is scalp grease is a different kind. I have a gentleman's paste I apply to stimulate hair growth. Has a badger secretion in its illusory ingredients. I am a firm believer in the body of the mind, or the thinking body. A condiment of health can be a sign or wonder.'

Bent said nothing, apparently in agreement.

'Ye beg to differ. . .' the surgeon was still absorbing the contents of the published letter.

'Keep bear oil in my hair.'

'Bear oil? And does that too, promise miracles?'

'Promises sleekness.'

'Just like my hair oil, then.'

'Like your hair oil. But I think I want your youth. Every day you feed its hungry ghost. But your youth is gone. It went with your dead son. He took it as your gift to him.'

Clarke seemed to absorb this truth slowly. 'And bear oil?'

'That is different. It nourishes all, young, old. I will bring you some for your whorl.'

'Beg pardon?'

'You have a whorl in your thumb and at the top of your head, there.'

'Want some coffee?' The surgeon yawned and stretched.

'I'll take a cup.'

Clarke got up and lit a small stove, wiped out two tin mugs, unscrewed the coffee pot. 'Why do they take a scalp?' He did not look up as he snuffed the match. 'I read on Herodotus and the Scythians, the Spanish too, liked to scoop it off.'

'An omen shape of a scalp in the moon. Dark like a shadow the hair sweeps before you. Offered to the Thunder God. But that's just the scalplock, uncut. Tended to in boyhood, shaped and painted.' Bent spoke the images in fragments. 'The Pawnee talk of a *kicahúrusksu*: a scalped man or a ruined man. How he is alone and cannot return to his people. He lives in a cave with a buffalo altar and sage scattered across the floor. In this way he is always known as Scalped Man. If he revives on the field, it's a different story. Then he becomes holy.' He paused to take his coffee, blowing on its pungent steam, 'you're going to talk with Parmetar before Setangya comes to the fort again?'

'I aim to.'

'What do you make of all this?' said Bent, referring to the article.

'This here's either masterful propaganda, or contains some bit of embedded truth. Hard to fathom how a personal correspondence could warrant legitimate public reading material.'

'Perhaps it was his wife.'

They spoke for some time on the recent state of affairs and on the war and the surgeon enquired after the interpreter's father.

'He is strong,' said Bent, 'has always lived between places, between peoples.'

Then I listened as Bent recounted how the Winter Count of sixty-two, sixty-three, was the Winter the Horses Ate Ashes. How Kiowa people camped up at Walnut Creek near the Red Sleeves River, struggled to keep themselves and their animals alive. How Eayre and Bowing and Chivington were much at fault for repeated antagonisms that past year of sixty-four and planned fresh attacks, all for making their names in the reputations of war. How the killing of Little Bear nearly caused a war itself, only Black Kettle stopped it. Then Bent's people, the Cheyenne, had camped near the Apache and Comanche, with the Arapaho and Kiowa a little way off, closer to the fort. His own father had drawn the chiefs together to have a talk there a few weeks ago. How most of the Cheyenne had moved southward to avoid trouble. Yet, there was no hope of any such parley with Captain James Parmetar and how time was wasted on such a purpose.

'Yes,' Clarke rubbed his eyes, 'Parmetar is dead weight to us, but perhaps he can be cautioned. I wonder if we don't need him here a while longer with things as they stand.'

'This goes further back than Parmetar —'

'Which merely endorses my argument.'

'No,' said Bent and continuing persuasively, told Clarke how rancher George Peacock had once betrayed Kiowa chief, Setangya with a false character reference, requested by Setangya to give an official endorsement of his good standing. So far as the chief knew it, this was agreed and it was written out. But the letter of introduction clearly stated the opposite: that Setangya was not a good man. Peacock presuming all the while that the old Kiowa would never possess the language to discover the true meaning of the letter contents.

'That broke the trust,' Bent said. 'The trust and all in it. That lie cost Peacock his life.'

'And so,' said Clarke, 'what is expected of me in all this?'

'The wagon train attacks of late have been bad, but are provoked. People are retaliating in the only way they know how. Setangya's son came: An-pay-kau-te (to you, Frank Given) came and spoke with me and said the attack here came after the Kiowa Ragweed Sun Dance and then the Victory Dance. Fort Larned shut its supplies off on general orders from Parmetar who did not tell Setangya or any of the other friendlies. They came down as usual, to collect their due. Setangya went to speak with Parmetar and tried to cross the line. He never knew not to come down to the post for supplies as previously agreed. Had always come down to the post before. One of his warriors saw the outlook sentry raise aim as they approached. He stepped in to protect his chief. The sentry had shouted "no, no, no" but Setangya was not made aware of this new rule about not approaching the fort.'

'As ever,' said Clarke.

Bent continued: 'When the soldier raised his rifle, Setangya quickly shot arrows in defense. None hit the mark. Three, I think. But the warrior with Setangya did shoot the soldier with his own arrow. Not a bad wound. But that's when the trouble started. Setangya's young men took several hundred head of Larned's oxen, but now I hear Setangya has told them to return the livestock. He understands it was a rash action. So, all this has brewed up in the trouble at Barrett's wagon-train.'

'I see.' Clarke slammed the stiff drawer he had opened to fetch out a sheet of writing paper. 'Carry on,' he said, and started a letter.

Bent watched him, as if in understanding. 'Seems there was Setangya's young men but maybe some others too. I can't be sure yet. It started as a friendly parley. They came up to the herd, then walked the ponies down the line. Shook hands with all the whites. Brockman said the freighters only had two weapons on them in the entire train. Said the other gun belonged to wagon master, Jerome Crowe, and that it misfired, he thinks, and then the whole thing started. You had a unit sent from here, buried ten. Two blacks together and then Beabee and his son. Seems the soldiers from Fort Zarah tried to get to them, Captain Dunlap tried, but he was cut off. Says he thinks the thing a decoy, that the boys were there to lure out the troops. I don't know about that. Anyway, a whole lot of flour sacks got ripped up and some supplies were taken. Shot an ox in the yoke with arrows and, in all, drove off most of the herd. Then, well, you know the rest. Seems the Larned soldiers took it upon themselves to perform a desecration. Things were looted, too. Don't know if you heard about that?'

The surgeon nodded his head. 'I heard about the looting.'

'Young Kiowa boy killed out there.'

Clarke stopped writing and put down his pen. 'I had hoped McKenny's visit last month would improve things. In my understanding, he had already written to Curtis saying that if there was not considerable care and the tribes treated better, then a general war on the plains would ensue, or words to that effect. But with a rancid, dilapidated, ill-equipped and collapsed fortification that was only ever quarter-constructed in the first place, now commanded by an inept and violent drunk who not only neglects his duties but prefers to stage ostentatious and unnecessary buffalo hunts that tire out and disquiet the horses, we are now in a situation where communications have terminally broken down between this agency and those tribes which it purports to serve. The result of this has been an attack on Barrett's supply train in direct retaliation. That about right?'

'That about sums it up,' said Bent, 'in addition to the ongoing lack of food, continual encroachment by whites and broken agreements, understandings, between government men out here and local chiefs. Place is ripe for petty bureaucrats and war thieves. Rest it on Parmetar's shoulders and you'll see he's a living embodiment of official betrayal. Most likely came out here to escape the war. You know yourself it's the laziest way to build a reputation. Turn prairie governance and rationing into a more exciting game through deliberate starvation of the tribes, push them into retaliation, and you chalk up a name as an Indian fighter, so-called. You push people. I seen it happen time and again. It ain't difficult to hand out hard tack and flour quarterly. The man is making a serious situation. Word is, war's brewing up out here. And he has a hand in it to answer for.'

'All right. Ye've my mind made up to send this dispatch for Parmetar's immediate discharge,' said Clarke, wearily. 'I'm commending him for fruit-farming. It will be sent as soon as I'm able on the morrow.'

'It *is* the morrow,' said Bent. 'What'll you do with those boys?'

'Heal them, I hope. One's perilous all the same. They're young — almighty young for droving. One is an orphan. He doesn't talk a great deal, but that much he has told me. Has sustained a bad head wound. Needs continuous rest and ongoing supervision. He should make it through. The injury covers so,' Clarke showed with his hands the area of damage. 'They're calling it a scalping'

Bent looked taken aback. 'That's too big a swatch for a scalping. When you take a scalp, it's small. About a dollar size right at the top of the head. Where the hair whorls. Here,' he spread both hands palm-upward on the desk, 'you can measure from lobe to nostril, hairline to eyebrow, wrist to elbow, knee to ankle and none will be so telling as this here thumbprint. You have a spiral in your thumb and at the top of your head, here. Your shadow moves, your voice moves, your blood moves, even your skin travels, but this here thumbprint is both moving and fixed, like a stilled tornado. Exact same on your head up where the hair grows from that place. Touch it, and you can feel the ignition point down your whole body as if it were the top vertebrae in your spine.'

'I do see that,' the surgeon said.

They conferred a while longer on fort matters mostly until, at length, the talk dwindled and Bent got up. 'Want me to take that dispatch for you? I'll pass it on to Jack Burd. Should get there safe.'

Clarke swiftly signed his name to the letter and sealed it down hard. 'Obliged,' he said, handing it over.

Bent nodded, folding the missive in the inner lining of his coat and said: 'There was a Spanish coat of mail given to us in exchange for horses. It was a suit of iron scales. Each scale was about the size of a half-dollar. They were sewn into a leather shirt. Any warrior wearing that old armor suit could wrap himself up in a scarlet blanket to hide the chainmail. Then he was bullet proof. Appearances can fit the nature of description, but sometimes a symbol is no good. You cling to a stale symbol to stall or hinder reality.'

Bent departed then, donning his soft hat, more a shape in the fort than a man. And as he went, the next day came. Out there in the first light, among those splintered spokes and abandoned wheels, stretched on a wheel bed no longer sprung with coils, I saw odd wagon contents scattered wide among the floury grasses: the cracked jar of a kerosene lamp glittering with dew, an iron grease-pan red in the dawn and half the contents of a narrow box: part-wood, part-bone dominoes, a ghost gamble spilled on the cold soil.

V

SÉANCE: E.E. HENRY PHOTOGRAPHIC STUDIO, LEAVENWORTH

Familiar spirit: H.H. Clarke, surgeon

CRYSTAL FLAKES THICKENED CLARKE'S yellowed storm glass, night after night, as if haunted by snow. And I strained to hear his roughened voice as he clasped that globe in hands equal-rough also, embittered by the late September's moon: 'ten weeks now and no reply to my report: James Parmetar remains in post.'

Then I glimpsed in the sphere of the surgeon's orb, his young patients slumbering — convex boys in crystalline woods. A small world asleep in a shimmering ball. And his own features morphed, gibbously reflected in hoary nitrate as he put the storm globe down with calculated stealth.

'Must get them moved on. To heal up at another site, escape the pending outbreak.'

The scene, rippling, then changed. I witnessed the careful surgeon laboring in a ward of soldiers he treated with antimony for vomiting and mercury as a laxative. There had been cupping, blistering, morphine ingesting.

'Though the men keep their infections close,' he said — sitting late and worn in the makeshift supplies room, the room which shaped his thoughts by lamplight — 'pneumonia means these boys must be evacuated.' He looked down, making feverish notes now: the indecipherable scrawl of an amateur medium.

Then in came a new spirit, a soldier who reported remains found in the arroyo down near the woods. 'Decayed some,' the soldier said, reluctant with a certain superstition that some of the rot had rubbed off on him.

When they brought in the corpse, Clarke said he knew whose it was from the letter still clutched in its fiercened grip. Recognized his own erratic hand on an envelope addressed to a General Curtis: discerned his own dispatch, insistent on Parmetar's removal from post.

And the body was lightly tipped in blood where the interpreter's throat had been raggedly cut with the broken shard of a fort's shattered windowpane. That shard which had lain in the grass, glittering, was now presented to the surgeon. And Clarke said he should have known, before his storm-sphere blossomed with the lightness of death, before its circumference kept a stained-glass blade, before that blade (as if artfully crimsoned, as if Massachusetts chapel sanguine, as if Judas' mouth or the whore Mary's hem) was shucked from its frame by a wind-blown, chipped stone, and made ready for its ill-found role as fatal incision-maker of the spirit's mind, the land's body of flesh. But Burd's footprints never showed up in that miniature world of bad weather. Like the storm globe, they shaped nothing but the premonition of a world underblown, a glass still liquid in its primary intention, as if still in part a great hot sea churning in its own demise; a sea, you could say, of un-pre-destined blood like so many bloods already taken in by that ground in the surge of overtake by milling greed; relentless claims on a land that would upsurge its truer people to die for it in a last outworking of that land's body: beyond stone, beyond water, beyond fire. That was the calumny of it, his death. That one caught in the great molten wash of wills that surged between territories of the wind made human, one who was made as liquified solid — not just in his anatomy, but in the absolute merging of his peopled cognizance

— might be culled in the ire of imposter will: say, the trenchant solidity of pioneer. That Jack Burd, stumbling from sleep in the morning half-light, who was prepared to pull the liquid cloak of the land around his shoulders, should be slain in that half-sleep, and not slain was the true seed, grain of sand, or grit mote of the violence of will itself. Clarke knew it. His spherule had blackened. He slated Burd in for burial by bird song, a lone white marker on a military plot. Then put into motion the long crossing.

'Yes,' he said, turning back to me now, 'I have no other proposition, have urged we send those juveniles to Fort Wise for the winter under military escort. That escort will then continue to Fort Union with James Parmetar, freshly dismissed from his command as captain of Company H, Twelfth Kansas Volunteer Infantry, for habitual drunkenness and held under suspicion on a charge of suspected murder for ordering the death of interpreter Jack Burd. McMullen can deal with him as he sees fit.'

Clarke conferred on this with Larned's first lieutenant, who said: 'We have the captain in irons, clapped up back there in the barracks room. Seemed keen to get himself into them. Strange thing, the sudden absence of liquor, the way it'll take a person. That trail's going to be hard-going for these boys.'

Clarke persisted, saying pneumonia would more surely kill them, that there was an almighty risk to the fort of attack since Burd's own violent death, that Parmetar's presence riled up the men, that neither he, nor the first lieutenant, had the authority to keep the captain in chains for any extended period of time and that Parmetar, given the motive and his previous conduct: 'Must now be taken on and dealt with properly under the aegis of Fort Union, sir.'

The first-lieutenant conceded: 'I can only spare three men for the full leg down to Union, along with your young acting nurse.'

And so, there was now enough evidence to have fresh paperwork stamped, folded and added to Clarke's original letter, prised from the envelope clenched in Burd's fist. The first lieutenant instructed a private Abraham Tunks to convey this missive on his person and to deliver it up to General McMullen before anything else — before anything else, mind — when they arrived at the fort. Then he briefed the men on the route, the forts, the watering points. They would get to the cut off fork, ride on up the Mountain Branch to Fort Wise, deliver the boys, have the mules looked over and watered, the supplies replenished and were then to go on to Fort Union with Parmetar kept under close guard.

The following morning the prairie fort lay still as a monastery, somber and still slumbering in the first faint flush of dawn. And I watched as the prisoner was roused from his sleep to dress and doubly cuffed. He was soiled and unkempt. They gave him coffee and grits and his bundled affects: among them a coyote bone toothpick and the carte-de-visite of a turbulent-looking young woman, worn to an almost-nothingness. There was the faint trace of a likeness in that turbulence. His own face was troubled by violence. He had a wan complexion, and his grizzled hair was overgrown, but as a last courtesy to his former rank, his stubbled jaw had been freshly shaven so that he looked pockmarked by black pepper. I saw he struggled as the alcohol left him, how in the end they had to feed him his breakfast. The coffee kept knocking out of its tin mug with his shuddering.

('He'll be no use to ye with hallucinations. Ye must roll it off,' said the surgeon to Hanna. 'No use making him dry at once. Give it him just little a day, then make it less and less.' And he gave the nurse a vial of brandy with a small pipette to lace Parmetar's coffee with. 'Don't let the other men see ye. Nor the captain himself.')

As they bundled the captain onto a horse, he asked that the irons be loosened off, but nothing was done for his manacled wrists. He waited as the darkness paled, head lowered to chest, as if deep in prayer. Waited, shaking, as they loaded up. I saw he carried a clenched destiny and knew of it, deep within himself. Chafed and withdrawn, he suffered a resigned endurance. And when the garrison troops drilled at dawn in a scant parade to see them off, he raised flinty eyes to survey his men, hard-stared back at the ranks with a defiant expression. A US army flag fluttered behind him, stuck in his saddle pack, its canton faded to a urinary yellow, as if those thirty-four stars shone dirty with fear.

Nearby, an ambulance-wagon was being fitted out with medical supplies, readied and equipped for the recuperating children. Fresh straw lined the Yankee bed with layered blankets arranged in between. I now watched as the two young patients were carried out and laid on this crude mattressing under more rough, woolen army blankets and the soft, heavy hides of buffalo.

Clarke motioned to me then and reluctantly, I joined them.

We were packed in tight between cordwood and bundles of jerky, water containers, kettles and flour sacks. Ammunition boxes swung from bows above the boys' small heads, bumping with each slight creak of the frame as the mules pawed the ground in their harnessing. The same smells of wood and dust and leather and jute were familiar to me from Crowe's wagon. I sat at the rear with a good view of the outside world and was glad to hunker right down in the wagon bed, wedged in by hides on a thick wad of blankets.

'Go easy now.' Clarke leaned into the back of the wagon, his breath like a bull's, clouding in the half-light. 'Sleep most of the way, if ye can. Ye boys are in good hands, I have drafted Hanna to tend ye, minister to all thy needs.'

The boys nodded mutely, their faces pale in the kerosene lamp light. Standing by Clarke, another spirit addressed me, saying: 'Ned Jones. I was grown up a bellows boy for a west Nebraska cartwright. Knew much from a young age of saddlery and wheel-craft, horse tack and bullet-making. Am a good handler of mules, handy with a shotgun. I died this month, Fall 1864.'

Jones had a closed face which would have been nondescript except for the ire in him that shaped a certain determination. I watched as he moved off toward Parmetar, tethered to Jones' own wagon.

'Seen a few campaigns, that one,' said the surgeon to me. 'Don't cross him.'

Jones checked over his captain, exchanging a few words, and double-checked his handcuffs and that the reins were securely tied to the pommel and that the horse's tether was well-secured to the wagon-frame. Then he mounted the wagon box, untied the mule reins and sat with them bunched loosely in his hands, waiting for the first wagon to finish the load-up with freight.

'Private Abraham Tunks,' said Clarke, 'mans the supplies wagon. He's that fellow over there, a rawboned night-gazer. Follows the whippet star.'

At the front of the train an older soldier lifted grain sacks, bacon, bullets and hard tack, biscuit, beans and dried fruit into the rear of the wagon. Spry for his age, he swung a small whisky barrel in with ease.

'He'd be eighty now, if he'd survived this trip,' Clarke said. 'Was prematurely aged, with merciless moods. Not a good harmonica player, as I recall, not a bad fiddle player. Liked sharp cards, would always lay down a bit or two. Had good sight, but went blind in one eye. Was a good rider and a good shot. Knew that trail like no-one else. He'll stand ye in good stead: show ye what occurred. Ah,' said the surgeon, 'now here's Abner Jameson. He'll join ye to drive this wagon. A good cook, Abner. Will ensure ye don't starve.'

The wagon lurched as Jameson got up and settled himself. He had a weatherbeaten face that was half-resigned and half-merry: with a strange twist in the mouth, but his voice was warm. 'Morning,' he said, and from the back Hanna murmured a reply to him.

'You see,' said the surgeon, 'the first lieutenant selected these three souls to accompany Hanna. They were colleagues and recruits, rather than friends, and if they'd remained so, the commission would have gone easier on them. And so they should have, so they should have done. At any rate, it shifted them all from pleurisy's path: detained death a little longer. Now go easy,' said the surgeon to his glassy-eyed boys, 'and don't forget to write me when ye get to Fort Wise.'

He stepped back as the call came: 'All's set!'

Then Tunks quirted up the lead mule and in the cold dawn made a start. Jameson followed, manning our ambulance-wagon. Jones' vehicle took up the rear, leading the captive on his tethered horse. Buried deep in his greatcoat, the prisoner looked like a bundle of jute hummocked on his saddle as steadily we drove on out. And in his mind's eye, I knew the surgeon watched over us, care crystallizing his sightline like those weather-foreboding chemicals formed in his static glass.

VI

SÉANCE: E.E. HENRY PHOTOGRAPHIC STUDIO, LEAVENWORTH

Familiar spirit: J.R.R. Hanna, nurse

I HAD NEVER BEEN so far west outside of this vision, had only absorbed the direct experience of my sitters at the photography studio, whose faces entrapped a vista of this outlying country, whose eyes were stamped with a high, blue prairie sky that was then imprinted on fresh paper. Now I understood their longing: it was a vista of pulmonary gentleness — a landscape which we breathed through the heart.

We were a small train of three wagons each drawn by a four-strong team of sturdy mules. Hitched to the last wagon, Parmetar jogged along with his hands still cuffed, on the back of a buck stallion. His tethered, penitential form appeared and disappeared behind us like a religious apparition in the clouds of billowing dust made by our catenulated boxes as they trundled along on their iron-clad wheels. We could have been a medieval unit of errant soldiers, knights or monks as we followed the Cimarron river's course whose grasslands were supple, undulant in a shot silk of pale green and pale yellow. Those soft grassy dunes that flanked us in a rippling ocean, rolled away to the far horizon and for mile after mile my eyes ached to look at them, but my mind grew softened. Never had I known such softness, as if the land were whispering to itself. Exhaustion rocked us, ongoing, as if we were the roped and tarpaulined matter of tiredness itself, pulled along by a jostle of mules; that the mules themselves, postured in weariness, jolted along with us caught behind, wearied as a worn rein, or a flapping blinker, or an old, dried cottonwood branch caught in the ragged tail husks of the creatures. The vaulted wagons jounced and rucked and were spattered with rain and powdered with dust, creviced with small veins of mud when the hail-storms came, and sat dankly recovering dryness when a heavy morning frost laid its cloak on the camp, or when rain sotted their awnings of jute. And disregarding all this, the grassland lisped and hissed to itself, whispering words of monotony and indifference, a language of the lightest touch.

Every day, it seemed to me, this land held open its cracked palm to our star-beleaguered crossing. In sleep, its fist clenched around my fitful dreams in which a recurring stranger loped a buffalo-field of bleached bones and sang into the night a high-pitched song that creased the calm of his face. Dust blew through his tendons and his heart gently smoked as his voice found its grain, and his pony tracks showed a world that slowly curved under the weight of dying. The whispering seemed to me then an interwoven curse and charm, of evoked and invoked threaded stems bound to a great nothingness whose pale air roiled through the atmosphere in a misshapen condition of smoke.

Every night, we corralled the wagons, slept out in the open, bunked around the cookfire's long-dying ashes that sprayed in the wind, as if under pressure. We corralled on the graves of wild mustangs: unmarked, unworried by inscriptions of passing. Our own livestock were watered along the river, their canteens refilled with its fresh-running water and on those banks I saw withered and frayed ghosts of dead herds that strayed and hovered and turned in historical dust-clouds, in clouds of rain, grit-hard showers and pummeling snow. And some cottonwoods there were spirits too, transparent in their spiraled grain, and chaste trees and black cherries, whose pellucid branches showed mile upon hundred mile of departed feathergrass: once burnt, cropped or otherwise deceased, evolving in it that seeded generation's experience of the movements of spirit deer and the insight of the specter of a breeze which now seemed to move our own breeze in a close-cropped shadowing.

Deer and antelope stood and grazed and ran and stood and ran and gazed, always watching. And bird life called us in the sifting wind. High above, the cooling air warped with the weft of wild birds and a clear silence fell beyond their pounding wings. I watched those flocks go over when we broke camp near the earth-crumbled bank of the steadily moving river.

When dawn roused us early each morning, the ground was the color of burnt sugar, thatched with those dewy, sage-colored grasses that glittered as the sun rose. We drained our bladders on that dark, weathered ground in the clear, weathered air, shiveringly lit the first fire, and brewed up bitter coffee that tanged of the earth's gall.

'Tastes like a bad conscience,' I heard Parmetar say to himself, but still he drank it down for the warmth.

We passed occasional stands of elm out there in those endless grasslands and the stark trees stood ashen-looking as the wind rose among them, whitening their branches with dust. When the first storms came they blew in hard, chunking hail into the noontime fire, stinging the mule rumps, bulleting our faces. Then just as fast, they blew out again. Rainbows splayed their watercolors in high, hard arcs across the deep gray sky whose clouds glowed oily in the banks of those thunderheads. Yet, there was another low rumble in that wide country, not of thunder stolidly waiting, cued by the flash of its cousin, but the thrum of thousand-upon-thousand-fold trundling wheels: a frequency of pioneer intent, scores of droving wagon hounds, reaches, jute-stretched frames and iron tires worn and wearing out. And my acumen tipped me off in a sudden flash, as if of said lightning, that still we only toiled in Clarke's stormy glass, that the hail would be false as if scattered from a rusty shaker of breadcrumbs, that the thinning and thickening of the glass of that globe, when once heat-sealed in tongs, would determine how much I could now fully hear, outwith the storm enclosed.

And so the vision kept on rolling out, kept straight and clear to its active ghosts, propelled within my normal sight. I surveyed them all closely now: their routines, their dynamics, as if sizing up each one before making a strong portrait. My fascination for them deepened in the camp-fire's bands of heat-thickened air as if in the congealed air of my own observation. Take Hanna: a juvenile nurse become dirty and thin. Had torn his coat in a thorn-thicket, out fetching up kindling. Face uplit now, in a dough of kneaded shadow. He was still good. Was wary of Parmetar, out there on a commission whose solitude pushed his discipline to some ever-distanced breaking point. Routinely, he administered morphine and daily, disposed of blood-soaked bandaging, burying it all in a shallow plot. Hanna, who proved wieldy with a weapon, who was slight and cautious and smart, who — with some presence of a three-quarter-tamed fox — still maintained a careful routine of cleanliness and healing, was himself profoundly heart-shocked. Yes, there was a thing fully unresolved about him: I saw he conveyed a constant fear within. But what better cure than to find the one who is damaged all the more.

'Morphine,' I'd heard him tell the smaller boy, way down the empty trail, 'will give you a wild old set of dreams.'

The young nurse now tended that boy's hurt skull with care, that care giving courage to both as Hanna unraveled the putrid lint, mixed up honey-water on the wagon tailboard, administered to his patient from an old wooden spoon, sang to him in a low and off-tune lilt, laid him back, tucked him in, said to himself: 'Still a child, no boy of thirteen — seems to exist in a permanent state of shuddering.'

I kept still in the dimness and watched him: juvenile, docile, vulnerable. Robert McGee, too young to be a drover yet. And Allen Edwards: feverish now in the long travelling, who yelled and clung to Hanna's sleeve when the pain got so bad. Edwards, the older of the two, felt it no less for the suffering.

That night I followed Hanna round the side of the wagon as he dried off his hands and crouched by the fire. His makeshift medical dispensing was done, the boys' tears dried, their traumas settled down. No infection threatened to blossom, only nightmares jeopardised healing. And in the meantime, darkness had fallen. Hanna's thin face was drawn in the flames, withered by sunburn, worn by traveling, but most of all that burden of fear seemed to trouble him.

'Seen to the boys?' Tunks handed him a tin cup: 'Careful.' He poured unsteadily.

'Want me to take a look at that?'

'Got it caught this morning in the jockey box.'

Hanna drank the coffee down. 'Nasty cut there. I'll fix you up after supper.'

Tunks nodded and passed him a dish of hot beans: 'Salt pork in it tonight.'

'Good,' said the nurse. He reached into the lining of his coat and pulled out a scuffed book. Sat with his right foot resting on his left kneecap and balanced the open volume on his boot so as to read it while eating in the flickering light.

'What you got there?' Tunks said, fork in hand. The tight skin on his haggard face shone, his mouth was drawn in a downturned line and his right eye rolled inward, unseeing. 'You a reading man?'

Hanna handed over the book to the gaunt soldier, who set down his plate and angled the cover, letting its embossed title catch the light.

'*A Companion to Common Prairie Flowers,*' he said. 'Let's see.' And he turned to a page and held it open, scanning the print with his one good eye: '*Asclepia, cleome, euphorbia, helianthus, malva, monarda,*' he read aloud, and his words sounded an uneven chant in the high, starlit prairie darkness. As he gently leafed through the translucent pages, a soft fall of pressed stems and dried wildflowers slipped silently into the fire's hungered and entangling flames.

'All died back now,' said Hanna, without noticing. 'Cold's numbed them. Their seeds are asleep. Wish the cold would do the same for those boys. You heard him call out?'

'I heard him,' said Tunks. 'Got fear in his dreams. Wouldn't want to see what he's seen. That's a whole different kind of recollection.' He squinted at the book's index. 'You must've come across things. Weren't you drafted, before Larned?'

Hanna paused. Held mid-air, his knife flashed fire in its blade, but his young face looked soiled with hollows.

He conveyed to the darkness an old memory: a barrow of limbs floating in sight. An outrage in a cornfield. Rebels slaughtering an ambulance of the wounded, piercing them through with bayonets. First time he'd shot a man, the soldier wouldn't die, but bled out at his feet. Hanna stayed with him for near on eleven hours — consoled him, gave him his coat, soothed him into death. Took it sick to heart. Got out on a prairie fort posting.

'Don't talk about it much,' he said, and carried on with his eating.

'Going rabbiting tomorrow?' said Jones.

'I aim to,' Tunks replied, still reading. 'Plenty out there by way of meat.' He shut the book and passed it back to Hanna with a slight nod. 'We'll not suffer.'

'Break out your fiddle, Jameson,' said Jones.

'Got a few strings broken,' Jameson grinned. 'But I could my work my way around them. Let me finish up here, first,' he said, wiping out the kettle of beans. He whistled softly, collecting up platters specked with ash from the fire's windblown embers as the soldiers sat contentedly smoking.

'I've a proposition for you, boys,' Parmetar said, 'best mentioned ahead of the cut-off. Roll me a cigarette there, Tunks.' The shackles dug deep into the captain's swollen wrists and when he nudged his plate toward Jameson, he used both hands. They were grimy and chapped and involuntarily cupped, like the cupped hands of a destitute priest. Tunks rolled one for him and lit it up with a glowing stick-end.

'Obliged, Abraham,' the captain said, carefully taking it from him. Beads of sweat prickled his upper lip as he sat pensively smoking and the firelight flickered over his hunched shoulders. 'Loma Parda,' he said. 'Means the Grey Hill. I feel we'd be best heading on over there, down the Cimmaron trail. It's a faster route. Better for wintering.'

No-one answered him. A general silence resumed, but the

night air was constrained now by a light tension.

'We're to escort you directly to McMullen.' Jones tipped his coffee dregs onto the fire, 'no use conjecturing on Loma Parda, captain.'

Parmetar leaned backwards in his fetters, awkwardly reclining on a wadding of blankets they'd spread out for him across the hard, cold ground. 'Someone told me they have a drink down there,' he said, his rough voice fading to almost nothing, 'they call it Loma Lightning.' He looked up at them. 'Now, Loma's close to Fort Union. Turn me in there, if you have to. Make a detour, a —'

'What was that?' said Tunks.

A thinness rose in the Cimarron blackness.

'That one of your boys again, Hanna?'

'Don't believe so,' said the nurse, but he made to get up.

'Best go check,' said Tunks in a kindly voice.

'Is just a wolf or coyote,' Jones said, lighting up a cigarette.

'No — that —' said Tunks.

They sat quiet, listening out for it.

'I don't hear nothing,' said Jameson, and began to scrape off the plates.

'Well, it's probably just them boys crying again,' said Tunks, but Hanna reappeared, shaking his head.

'They're sleeping hard,' he said, without settling back down by the fire.

When it came again, Parmetar raised himself on an elbow. 'Quit that for a moment,' he said to Jameson.

'I'm nearly done,' he said, but stopped what he was doing.

A night wind flickered the prairie grasses, carrying the same distorted sound.

'Most likely a coyote caught in a trap,' said Tunks, pouring out another cup of coffee for himself.

But then the silence was broken again.

'It's getting closer,' said Parmetar. 'Help me up.'

Jones came round the campfire and got Parmetar onto his feet.

The cry came again.

'What in the hell is that?' Tunks got up now, brushing down his uniform jacket, creased from where he'd been sitting on it. He put it on, shivering as the scream came again.

'Sounds like a woman calling out,' said Jones. He stood with his back to the fire, staring out into the blackness.

When the scream came again, it was shrill and contorted and bestial.

'Undo me,' said Parmetar.

The soldiers stood motionless in the firelight.

'Undo me,' he repeated, sharply.

Tunks began to protest, hand on his weapon.

But when Jones spoke, his tone was even: 'Do as the captain says, Abraham.'

The soldier did nothing. No-one took the rusted hoop of keys he held out, so Jones found the key on the shank himself: 'Keep your aim on him, Tunks,' he said and moved in close to the captain.

'Raise your fists.' He carefully unlocked the manacle's solid heart of iron. The chains swung loose and Parmetar stood, touching his chafed wrists.

'Mind me,' said Jones, crouching down to release the captain's ankle fetters, 'if this prisoner gets riled, or runs, then it'll be me answers for it. Now, I'm about to undo these here ones. Got your aim on him?'

'This whole time.' Tunks cocked the hammer with slow determination.

Jones undid the lock and Parmetar stepped out of his chains. He stood, motionless and unspeaking.

'Whatever it is, the captain's right,' said Jones. 'It's coming closer and it's coming from the north.'

'Reckon you should get out there and find her?' Hanna said as Tunks and Jameson glanced at one another. He was still young, Jaspar Hanna.

'Could do,' said Jones. 'I think we should just stay holed up here by the fire. Except you, sir.' He motioned at Parmetar. 'You're going out there on a recce.'

The captain cleared his throat. 'All right,' he said, 'now listen. We're all set up here — we've got seven breech-loaders and a couple of colts stashed in the back there. We're much stronger staying put. Lose me and you're one man down.'

Jones was unmoved: 'I need someone to get out there and scout around,' he said, 'you've the most experience.'

Parmetar looked at him. 'Going to send me out unarmed?'

'For chrissakes,' said Jameson, 'give the man a weapon.'

'Gun or horse,' said Jones. 'Your choice.'

Parmetar considered this. 'I'll go it on foot,' he said.

Jameson removed some bullets from his colt and passed the pistol to the captain. 'You've got two shots at it.'

Parmetar tucked the pistol in his belt. 'Now get me a lantern.' he said.

Tunks passed it to him. Then the captain straightened his hat and walked out into the black milk of night.

FOR THE first half hour after his departure, my eyes strained in the darkness. I could just make out Parmetar's lantern as it quivered softly in the vast night, until finally its golden glow disappeared. There was a strong breeze which now and again lifted embers from the fire. Ash sifted in the air, turning in light flurries. Still burning flakes, blown upward from charred sticks, burnt away when they touched the flames again, and encircling the cookfire base was an aureole of powdered cinders that slowly thickened like a ring around the moon. I concentrated on these ash flakes, dissolving just within the fire's touch. Sometimes it got so this cinereal dance-in-darkness of softening white on licking gold, whirred wildly when the wind got up. Every so often, the wild cry came and each time it raised the hair on the back of my neck. Then silence fell again and I stared into the darkness, fixed on the point where the captain's light had vanished.

Jones had lifted out the remaining weapons from the supplies wagon, unhooking the bullet boxes. He loaded the rifles and passed them out. Then Hanna wakened the boys, showed them each how to fire a pistol and left the guns with them.

The four soldiers crouched, nursing their rifles. There was another blast of wind and flakes of ash wildly wheeled about in it.

'Damn cold,' said Jameson, pulling his coat closer around him.

'Feels like there's a real storm brewing,' said Jones. 'Keep that fire stoked.' He sat cross-legged on the ground with his back to the blaze looking out into the darkness, an old breech-loader resting in his lap. In the clear night air the mules stamped and lunged on their tethers as louder now, the scream came again. Then the air settled into silence as the great dark loomed, expansive and chilling, and void of sound.

'You reckon Parmetar was responsible?' said Tunks, presently.

'For what?' said Hanna.

'The interpreter. Rumor says Burd had the discharge letter on him.'

The arroyo-wood fire crackled and sparked as ash-soft, the wind changed direction.

'A man in his position would want to run,' said Jameson, shifting on his haunches. 'Strange he didn't opt for the horse. I would've gone for the horse and taken off.'

'You can pick up a horse if you've got a gun,' said Tunks. 'I'd have taken the weapon like he's done, hunkered down somewhere and waited it out. Then, if anything happened to us, he can get back and check on it come daylight. We might get wiped out. Then that'd save him the trouble of being pursued.'

'Save him the trouble of getting himself killed,' Jameson said. 'He's a sober man now, he'll figure it out. I heard he was a fine shot before Larned.'

'When he gets back, I want him straightaway cuffed and checked over for the colt,' said Jones, chewing on a tobacco wad.

'If he's coming back,' said Tunks.

'Won't get far in this darkness on his own,' said Jones, spitting on the ground and wiping his mouth. 'More likely, break an ankle. His kerosene lamp's the one run low.'

'He'd get far enough,' muttered Jameson. He got up and stood surveying the darkness. 'Someone might come along, pick him up.'

Then the scream came again, much closer now. There was something human trapped in the animal.

Hanna murmured incoherently, under his breath.

'Easy now,' said Jones. 'What do you see?' he said to Jameson.

'Not sure,' said Jameson, cocking the hammer on his pistol

to lighten the trigger weight. 'Not sure, but it's coming closer. There — see it?'

Jones scrutinised the darkness.

'Keep looking.'

'Got it,' said Jones and was up on his feet.

I squinted at the invisible horizon and saw a faint tint of light bobbing in the dark. We watched it grow for a full hour, sometimes invisible, sometimes re-emerging. It seemed a friendly light, until we heard the scream again. Eventually, high in the wind-scraped air, came the whinny of a horse.

'That's what I've been waiting for. We've got some riders. You give them boys morphine?' Jones said. He worked the tobacco wad relentlessly, pacing by the fire.

'I did,' said Hanna, getting up.

Things get bad I want you to go back there and take care of them. Do it through the blankets, that way they won't know about it.'

Hanna said nothing.

'They're coming in real slow,' Tunks said.

'Got all night ahead of them,' said Jones.

The raw scream came again, seeming to rip the air apart.

'Oh god,' said Hanna, short of breath as he started to pray.

'Ready, now,' said Jones. 'If it turns out bad for the captain, remember they'll just as likely hang him.' He was pouring sweat and I saw his fingers trembled as he handled his gun.

The fire roared and shaved and danced in-between us. Time slowed interminably as still we waited on.

Then I heard the faint jingle of tack, as steadily now, the light approached. There was a small glow beside it like blown glass and I could hear the lantern flame roar softly, as it flared in the wind.

Then the coruscating scream came again, right in among us this time. The fire flames seemed to congeal as a largeness crossed their heat. In slow time, a blur of torsion. In slow time, the men took aim. Bewildered, irreverent, dream-like with tension, the fire was an uproar of rippling silk.

'No —' came a sharp voice. A man stepped forward, gripping the end of a frayed rope in each fist. 'Don't shoot. She won't hurt you none.'

The stranger had a strong hold on both ropes, his knuckle bones pale in the flickering light, but Jones kept his rifle raised as a panther padded forward into the firelight.

With a short, hacking sound Jameson suddenly broke into laughter.

The man looked him over and coiled each rope end around his left and then right forearm. Then he carefully lit a pipe. His clothes were freckled with diamonds, stitched into silk in glimmering patterns. For a moment out there, he had looked like a traveling chandelier. Now he stood stippled with rainbows in the moving fire.

'Wearing it, so it don't get drowned. Back there on the horse, is my proper coat. This here's just my show-gear. Figured it might help scare any unwanteds off.'

He was dandified and dirty with whipped-up, oily, white hair, an unkempt beard and small, hard eyes. Looked like he'd been out on the trail a long time. His greased whiskers shone silver in the coppery light, as he sucked on the pipe clenched between his teeth and formally introduced himself.

'My name is Junius Browne,' he said. 'Out there's my show wagon. With the storm coming I ran into trouble. Saw the light from your fire a way off.'

'Where's Parmetar?' said Jones and I knew by his tone that the private aimed to hurt him.

In the outskirts of darkness, a thin mare stood on an extended tether. Browne yanked the horse nearer and Parmetar came in along with her, patting her flank and holding her bridle. He'd kept back a little, nursing his freedom and avoiding the panther. Must have sensed all the while how keyed up the men were.

'Found them down by the river with a bust-up wagon, half gone in the mud. Said we would help them.'

'Not for you to decide,' said Jones, divesting the captain of his weapon. 'Back in, sir,' he nudged Parmetar with his gun.

The captain held out both wrists as Jones locked the cufflinks. Then he stepped, one by one, into the open manacles and waited unspeaking, as Jones bent down to secure them. As Jones lowered the captain back to the ground again, Jameson rolled a fresh cigarette and gave it to the captain.

'Are you hurt, Dr. Browne?' the nurse spoke up, cool-voiced in the night air.

'Nope, but like he said, I got a wagon that's stuck in a creek about a half mile back and the wind's coming on fair fierce now. Need your help to shift her, if I'm going get her out of that water tonight.'

There was silence.

'I don't think it so wise for us to get caught up in a storm,' said Jones, after some moments' consideration.

'Seems to me you ain't got much choice,' Browne said and his pipe bowl glowed, 'as it's headed in this direction. You assist me in this, I shall give each man here, a dollar. My whole livelihood — ever thing I own's — out there on that cart. Got bullets and tobacco and spirits too, that's yourn for the taking.'

VII

SÉANCE: E.E. HENRY PHOTOGRAPHIC STUDIO, LEAVENWORTH

Familiar spirit: H.H. Clarke, surgeon

PARMETAR, BROWNE, JONES, JAMESON: those four saddled up and rode out leaving Tunks, Hanna and the boys alone in camp. I went with the four men as they rode out knowing it was not far in miles, but that distance warps in darkness.

When the river glimmered we slowed the mules to a halt and dismounting, found the wooden show wagon: its front-end sunk in the shallows, the falling-tongue stuck at a sharp angle. I looked on as the men got the rear-end roped and the horse hitched up. Then they tried to heave the wedged vehicle out of the rising creek, but every time they hauled it up the front wheels sank deeper into the slippery mudbank.

'Give it one more go,' shouted Jones. They whipped up the horse and pulled again and the air split with the sound of cracking wood.

'Quit!' shouted Jones. 'Okay, down there?' he called to Jameson.

The older man was down at the wagon front, standing in the shallows and had put his full weight against the doubletree, supporting it with his shoulder blade. Parmetar stood on the shale grasping a lantern on a pole to give the men some light and hail pinged off its glass like shrapnel.

'Got a saw?' Jameson shouted back, his voice strained with exertion, 'reckon we have to get the falling tongue off.'

'It'll be useless without the tongue — what's he gonna hitch it to?'

'Unsure,' panted Jameson, 'but it's cracked anyways. More it slithers down, more the neck yoke gets stuck in. Must've got caught between rocks on the riverbed. That there's your problem.'

'All right,' shouted Jones, 'now hang on, just hold on there,' and he waded round again to Browne, who had his horse held tight by the bit, and said, 'got a saw in the back there? Falling tongue's split and the neck yoke's wedged in the mud. We can loosen her off, if we cut it free.'

'What am I supposed to hitch her to?' said Browne. His oily hair was covered in hail droplets and the naked hand gripping the oil light was red-raw with cold. 'We'd be better off hitching up a mule or two to help out this here horse, and drag that wagon out with more pulling-power.'

'Well, whatever you decide, make it fast. This river's rising and the hail's getting worse. We can have that tongue off in a few minutes. Wants to come off, by the looks of things.'

Browne paused a moment. 'I'll fetch the saw.'

Jones waded back down into the water, gasping, with the saw held high above his head. The men had the horse continually whipped and with her constant strain she held the wagon in place, but the wagon nose lifted in the currents swirling with motes of ice. Jones passed Jameson the saw. 'Can you stay on in the water and work it? You're faster than I am. I'll get up to the bank and hold it. Brake block's gone.'

Jameson shouted: 'Yes.'

'Mind the shaft end when you get through the tongue, it might shunt all of a sudden. Keep back when you're near, you hear me?

Keep back when you're close to cutting it clean through.'

Jameson watched as Jones waded to the bank and got up it, half-crawling. Saw him put his shoulder to the wagon bed. Then he found the bevel and worked the wood above the split, which was slightly submerged, worked it hard, but the grain was soaked and the saw-teeth slipped and caught, slipped and caught, resisting any real take on the wood.

'Faster,' shouted Jones, 'I can't hold it much longer.'

'Nearly there —' cried Jameson, but there was another shout and a wrench, as Jones called out and the cart lurched forward. A panel sprang open and bottles flew into the river water.

At the back of the vehicle, the men had felt the give as the horse reared up in the hail storm. Jameson steadied himself in the freezing water.

'All right, now,' said Jones. 'Let's switch. Get out now, you'll catch your death.'

'Wait a minute there, boys,' shouted Parmetar at them. 'This man needs a break. Let me step in here. Let me step in.'

Jones looked Abner Jameson over. He stood shivering, but his face was determined. He was older and so was stubborn. 'I can handle it, Jones,' he called.

Jones spat on the ground and wiped his mouth. 'You go on up to the bank now and undo the captain. Go on —'

With a groan, Jameson rolled out of position and Jones stepped in, taking the brunt of the rear-end. 'Quick,' he shouted, again realizing the full heft of the wagon. 'Can't hold it like this for too long.'

Jameson waded to the bank and hauled himself out, shuddering. He unshackled the prisoner and shouted for Browne to whip up the horse again and the wagon inched back in the mud.

'Let's start over,' shouted Parmetar, splashing into the freezing water. Jones stayed in his old position at the broken brake with the Yankee bed resting hard on his shoulder. He took its weight determinedly, with a clamped jaw, could see Parmetar working the saw fast, seemed to have a groove established and was working it over, back and forth. Soon they would be done.

Suddenly, the icy bank gave a little and the wagon pitched forward again. Losing his footing on the wet ground, Jones slithered back and cried out as the back wheel went over him. Then, there was a hard breach of wood as the tongue came free and the horse leapt forward in the reigns with a sudden light load but Jones was crushed as now the front wheel drove over him and Parmetar saw and plowed swiftly through the water and slithered up out of the river mud and crouched next to him, lifting his head off the ground. Jones' breathing was fractured and his crushed lungs came to the surface in bright blood that bubbled in a corner of his mouth.

'Couldn't hold it,' he said.

'Come on, now,' urged Parmetar, 'we're done, come on now.'

But Jones was already gone and Parmetar found himself holding a corpse.

'Get a blanket,' he said. He closed the soldier's eyelids with his thumb. Sat with him until Jameson dropped a blanket by the body and rolled some tobacco with shaking hands. Passed one to Parmetar and lit one himself. He stood looking out at the water, clouded in smoke. Browne hung about the wagon saying nothing. Parmetar laid the blanket over Jones and on the body of the dead man, found a holstered gun. When no one was looking, he wedged the pistol in the waistband of his pants. Then he rolled the body in the gray supply blanket and went over to the other men.

'What are you planning on doing with him?' Browne said, lighting his pipe again. 'No use trying to bury him. Ground's like stone.'

'Body like that'll bring a wolf pack in,' Jameson observed quietly.

'We'll float him downriver,' said Parmetar, after a moment's meditation.

They hauled Jones' body to the riverbank and in one motion, swung it into the water. The corpse drifted facedown, then hit a current and was gone.

It was over.

The wagon hauled out easily now without the resistant falling tongue and sat on the ground, dripping. Jameson put Parmetar back in his chains as Browne handed round a whiskey bottle, offered a dollar apiece to the ghosts of the men. One by one they took their share and swigged the spirits in silence, still shocked, still numb.

VIII

SÉANCE: E.E. HENRY PHOTOGRAPHIC STUDIO, LEAVENWORTH

Familiar spirit: J.R.R. Hanna

WE PACKED UP EARLY next morning, crossing a crisp vista, blue and luminous with bald patches of rock. The trail was hard-going for the first fourteen miles or so and no-one passed us until an overland mail wagon emerged from a hidden draw by the river. When the horse-drawn mail overtook, the roans caught the panther's stench as she rubbed the bars of her wicker-wood cage, and careened into an enclosure of rocks, upturning the stagecoach like a carton of eggs.

Fast-catching up to it, Jameson drew his mules to a halt and dismounted the wagon box, scratching his head.

Dust rose in the cold air. Thrown from his seat, the mail-carrier lay dead in the ravine far below and, as if in some Elizabethan play, a metaphysical-seeming flurry of paper-craft had come to circle, then land on his chest, like a quiver of arrow flights stripped by speed from their shafts.

Jameson, squinting at the body over the edge, said: 'That was reckless. Best hope he's dead.'

The soldiers lashed the horses to Parmetar's buck stallion and scooped up the missives, the packets and parcels, and with an ax broke up the stagecoach for firewood and set light to the letters. In three-quarters of an hour they were done.

'We'll set an early camp in that dead pine grove tonight,' said Jameson. 'Don't want to push these mules too hard.'

So, corralling the wagons, we raised a canvas tarpaulin for the livestock, drew water from the nearby creek, banked up a large blaze and gave the draft beasts their corn and feed.

Jameson walked out a bit before supper, into the high blackness. Took a cheroot with him and stood for a while smoking it right down to the bitterness. The others moved around the fire in torpid silhouettes, maneuvering kettles and pans. Tunks had wandered off to pass water, Browne to feed his panther, Hanna to check on the boys again. And so it was that in that moment, Jameson was able to crouch by Parmetar and softly confer with him. There was a low mulling between the two until the others wandered back to that sparking fire whose flames flickered indifferently. Tunks lumbered over, doing up his flies as he walked and Browne, joining the men, passed a whiskey bottle around to take the edge off their hunger. They were again settled in for the night.

Once more, the young healer had laid out his apothecary on the rough wood of the wagon tailgate as the smell of skinned rabbit on the fire co-mingled with smoke. Clambering into the dank box bed he found the boys slumped in blankets.

He looked Edwards over, concern in his eyes. 'How long has he been like this, Robert?'

'Since this afternoon.'

Hanna paused for just a moment. He was light and nimble and had a healer's timing in him.

'Hold still,' he said softly and Edwards obeyed. The lint came away unevenly, patched to pain by blood and the boy cried out.

I watched as Hanna swabbed and cleaned the wound and wrapped it up in fresh lint but the boy looked even paler now beneath the fly-haunted oil lamp that evicted ripples of heat above its glass spout. Outside, the air thickened with smoke as laughter rose among the sparks of crackling firewood. Now Hanna gave them each a dish of porridge to eat and sugared coffee with a stirring spoon. Edwards' lark-small skull had a shrunken quality to it: his sunken eye-hollows were pooled with feverishness. Both boys had a pall over them, as if kept in childhood bodies envenomed by experience.

'I'll fetch you both a hot stone,' the nurse said presently, testing the dampness on the older boy's forehead. 'Lay yourself down now.' And he drew the rough army blanket over Edwards and the boy pushed away its roughness, irritated, before he settled back into morphine.

From outside, the smoke-wreathed conversation drifted through the wagon awning. We were just in earshot of their fire-heated talk.

'There's limited money in traveling bones, emanations, villains, mer-folk and such like. Back there in the wagon, I've got flame-changers: epsom salts to make the fire turn white, Condy's crystals and copper sulfate and calcium salts and some strontium, all for making multicolored fires with. I've got chalk pastilles, snake venoms, hemps, powders, syrups to wash hands of flesh and dust. Blood bitters, prickly ash bitters and drops. Mineral salts for pox. Tonics for the broken heart and hard-toiling spirit. I was a military embalmer before being a showman. There's good money in war preservation. It'd cost one hundred dollars if you want a colonel done. Privates, like yourselves, would fetch one five dollar bill apiece. Brigadier-general, two hundred.'

'How d'you do it?' came Tunks' voice, slurred in the clear air.

'Well, it takes roughly five pounds of pressure to embalm a body in five hours. We used to use a door laid out flat on two casks to drain them. But there's often no need if a soldier's bled himself out on the field. That makes things easier, then. You've got a rubber ball and a tube and you pump in special fluid. I've got my own patent, but most use what's known as Holmes Solution. You've got your heavy metals in it, your mercury and zinc, sugar lead, soda iodine, phenol and some alcohol. Some use creosote. Then you've mostly got arsenic in it, something like from three quarter arsenic to ninety percent. Some others also concoct their own and sell it on, well that's like Holmes Solution.'

'Ever tried to embalm yourself?'

'I knew a man called Beauregard who'd tried to embalm his left hand with a tourniquet clapped around the wrist. It had turned necrotic from a dog bite and he thought to test out his fluids on it. Died the following day.'

After a while, the men from the campfire moved away again toward Browne's stationed show wagon and the laughter grew faint.

Hanna returned with the hot stones and tilted the base of the kerosene lamp suspended from the wagon joist.

'Give me that bowl if you're done with it. You done?'

Hanna took the other bowl and twinned them in an uneven pile and turned to the younger boy, Robert, who looked up at him with resigned expectation.

'Ready now for your turn?' Hanna said. 'Be as gentle as I can.'

And the lint unrolled in clots of anguish but the boy, bright-eyed with tears, stayed steady and his nurse worked swiftly, deftly, for the two were near but not the same, and worked his timing into healing, knowing when to pull suddenly and when to ease right back. In time, the bandage came away as a scroll of pain, a history of the boy's bright suffering. But this was only the unveiling. Hanna lightly pressed ointments around the opening, soaked the lint in astringent and wrapped the boy's shaven head with a rhythmic craft. Time was bound in with healing and the boy stayed still as if to in-soak Hanna's soothing touch. When Hanna removed the bite stick still clenched between Robert's teeth, the boy clasped it to his chest like a rudimentary crucifix whose cross bar had come apart.

'Done,' said Hanna, sounding the end. This, their routine each evening.

'Now get some shut eye,' he said and hung up the lantern before blowing it out. There was quiet. Hanna paused for a moment, then left.

IX

SÉANCE: E.E. HENRY PHOTOGRAPHIC STUDIO, LEAVENWORTH

Familiar spirit: James Parmetar

UNDER AN ASHEN SUN, I watched them lay the dead boy out: the old soldier who wrapped him in an empty grain-sack after the young nurse had straightened his childish limbs. His face had a slack blankness to it apart from a frown-line worked in deep through pain. I'd seen it before, that aura of exhaustion, that pallor from a hard-won death. He'd had chapped hands, Allen Edwards. I remembered those hands, still clenched as they sewed the seed sack closed.

The men stood around, quietly smoking.

'Bob know?' asked Tunks.

Hanna dazedly shook his head: 'Still sleeping,' he said and took the offer of a cigarette.

'You gave him a calmative?'

Hanna nodded, coughing, and handed the cigarette back to Tunks who wandered away and stood apart, smoking it.

'Best think now on how to dispose of him,' Parmetar said, approaching with Jameson.

They considered this for a short while.

'Wolves will likely be drawn in by the smell,' said Jameson. 'We can't take him down to the fort. Too many dead now with Jones there in the river water. Some sort of genocidal instinct out here among us, they'll think, and they'll always now think to pin it on you, captain. I say we refresh the horses, replenish our water containers and reroute to the Cimarron Cut-off. Then detour as we near Fort Union, and make it over to Loma Parda.'

'I was thinking on Loma myself,' said Browne. He stood in clouds of cigar smoke. 'They have the death carnival down there: we can make it. My best thought is to preserve the boy, honor him in his death-hood by making of him a small display. A fine and worthy spectacle. I have just enough fluid to do it.'

Hanna's voice was high now and shrill, and his breath was short with tension.

'You'll not touch Edwards,' he said, 'and I'll not go on with you to Loma Parda. The other boy needs rest and treatment, and he'll get both up at Bent's Fort. We can break the journey and they'll see to the mules there. I say we part with you, Browne, at that point.'

'You, Jameson?' said the captain, now turning to the other soldier.

'If I had my druthers, I'd go for Parda,' Jameson said, and spat on the ground.

Then Tunks came over, patting the paperwork in his coat lining. 'I will swear by you, captain,' he said, 'but I must do it in front of those who'd listen. If we digress, my soldiering's on the line.'

'Now think on it, Tunks,' said Parmetar, 'this here's a split party: there's three who'll aim for Loma and two set on the fort.' He shuffled in his chains: 'I'm going to ask around again. Browne?'

'Loma, as I said.'

Jameson?'

'Loma.'

'Hanna?'

'I'm with Tunks. Following orders. We've started up the

Mountain Branch, there's good water, places to bunk. Fort Bent's a good stop-off. Otherwise we have problems: water's a problem. I'm with you, Tunks.'

'Get into the back of that wagon,' said Tunks to Parmetar, hand on his weapon. 'Jameson, I'll take it you're just weak-minded. I'll take it you want to follow orders and peel your destiny from the captain's. Otherwise, we can sling you in the back, too. We've got to get on down to McMullen. Fort Wise is the destination. The Mountain Trail. Get set,' he shouted to the air, walking off toward the dying cookfire, 'we're on the move in a quarter hour.'

Jameson shrugged and spat on the ground and moved in toward the captain. Tussling with his belt, he pulled out the hidden colt. Parmetar remained motionless. Then he understood, and took the weapon and shuffled over to the fire and as Tunks looked up, shot him in the face. Then he took aim and shot Hanna in the back as he raced across the cold, dark ground. The nurse crumpled in the double-stride of a slow run. Parmetar sank right down on the hard-packed earth and listened to the sound of his own light panting, as the pistol slipped from his trembling hand

Browne emerged slow from his wagon, both arms raised.

'Ain't you,' said Parmetar, without looking up.

The embalmer came over cautiously, sat down by the fire and lit his pipe. He sucked on it for a long moment. 'What're you wanted for?'

The captain sat, unmoving.

'Drinking,' Jameson spoke up for him, 'murder, and wrestling a firearm off of Jones' corpse.'

Browne considered this. 'And are you guilty?'

Parmetar looked directly at him.

Browne cupped the pipe bowl in his palm. 'So, Loma Parda,'

he said, and passed a bottle of rye around.

'Loma Parda,' repeated the captain, as he took a swig. 'There's a key for these irons on Tunks.' He gestured with his shackled hands.

Browne got to his feet and went over to the corpse. Tunks' upper body lay slumped forward across his knees and the back of his skull was a mulch of blood. Browne clenched the pipe in his teeth as he fumbled about in the dead man's clothes.

'Nothing here,' he said, but discreetly pulled the packet from Tunks' overcoat.

Parmetar looked up. 'Hanna must have it.'

The nurse's body lay a little way off, a dark heap on the ground. Browne went over to it and trudged back to the fire with the key. 'Got your paperwork here, but I'll keep a hold of it in case you're of a mind to shoot me.'

'Were I of a mind to shoot you, papers wouldn't stop me. Keep the gun on you, if you're concerned. Here —' Parmetar picked up the spent colt and held it out.

'I'm just grateful we camped in a swale,' said Browne, ignoring the gun. 'No curious folks, passing.'

A light rain began to fall and the wind lifted the dust so that it puckered and was pounced.

'Hail's going to come down hard again,' said Browne, seeing to Parmetar's cuffed hands. 'We'll suffer by it if we don't get started.' His hair now clung in rats' tails to his forehead and droplets of water hung from his earlobes like diamond earrings. 'That's you free,' he said, as the captain stepped out of his ankle chains.

'We should wait it out,' said Jameson, standing nearby, watching them, smoking. 'I'll get a tarpaulin up. We should eat first and then decide what to do with them.'

I watched as Jameson rigged up an awning and relit the fire and got a pot of coffee going and a kettle of beans on and lay down for a while, silently smoking, as the arroyo-wood licked into light. The other two looked on, exhaustedly watching him prod the fire, but no heat warmed them from its immolating branches.

'I DON'T like to do it,' Jameson was saying uncertainly, 'I don't want no part of that.'

The rain was falling harder now in sudden, wet little gusts and there was a sting of cold in the air.

'Well, we only need two wagons and a cart. Could leave the other one,' Parmetar said. He passed the whiskey bottle to Jameson.

'We could,' said Browne. His small eyes focused, viper-like. 'I should have liked to prepare them, but there's not enough fluid. We work swiftly now: Parmetar you'd best strip the nurse and Jameson, do the same for Tunks.'

The soldiers took another long drink of whiskey each and Parmetar made a track through the clinging wet grass to the spot where Hanna lay face-down. He stood for a long moment, then he took the body by the shoulder and turned it over and began to strip Hanna's corpse. The buttons were slippery and stiff as he pressed each one through its damp button-hole and peeled the blood-stained jacket off. It lay cast-off in the grass, set in its shape — still molded to the heat and smell and life of the man it had bonded with, still soft in the underarm sweat, in flecks of frayed bandage trimming, one button half come-off that Hanna had been meaning, night after night, to sew on. His jacket sleeve was still torn from wood-gathering and there was another, small blood stain on the left arm from McGee's head wound, near a burn-mark when he'd balanced the coffee pot on his forearm and it had singed the fabric clear through. Parmetar watched as a fly crawled over the nurse's eyelid and across the dead film of his pupil and eye-white, to nest in the tear-duct, rubbing its hind legs. He flicked it off. Hanna's shirt and undershirt of soiled and bloody linen were now dampened by rain and Parmetar easily ripped them off. They fell apart in rags in his hands and he roughly turned the body over to strip one, and then the other arm, and came away holding what looked like a sopping and blotched flag of blood. He dumped it on the wet grass where it sat wetly in a mound, then he lifted the body in his arms and turned it again.

My first impression was of plumpness, of two small-mounded breasts, nipples swollen. Centre-chest was the ragged exit wound. Parmetar had a good aim. There was a pronounced collarbone on Hanna's slim-hipped form and Parmetar squatted, looking over the small body. Then, in one rough motion, pulled down the corpse's pants. It was nude beneath the rough cotton drill, pudenda furzed with a small bush of reddish hair, and that was all. On the ground nearby, hidden in the grasses, lay the blood-stained copy of the prairie flowers guide. Its gilt edges shone up palely, leached in the mid-morning light.

I watched as the captain buried his head in both arms for a good while, rocking back and forth. Presently he stopped and felt in his coat and brought out a small card with a woman's face on it and stroked this face with a blood-dried finger, stroked it and talked to it and then put it back, swiveling on his heel, as a crow battered upward from a tree, disturbing the lichen-lined branches. He stood up and scooped the pants and jacket up, laying them over his right arm, and chucked the rags over his left. Then he tied Hanna's bootlaces together and slung the boots over his shoulder. Picking up the small book, he carefully pocketed it. Then he gripped her body under the armpits and dragged it nakedly back toward camp. Her heels left a dark trail through the soft and bedraggled prairie grasses in-soaked with misting rain.

Parmetar laid Hanna's body next to Tunks' large-boned, aging corpse that suddenly looked defiled by death. The blood that had swarmed, was now congealed in his gray-haired skull. One by one, Jameson had dropped Tunks' undergarments on the well-stoked fire, turned them as they charred. But he kept the soldier's uniform for a change of clothes when the clean-up was done.

'I'll be damned,' he muttered, softly gazing at Hanna's slight body. 'I'll be damned.'

'Ain't right to defile the body of a woman,' Parmetar said. 'We should bury this one.'

'And you think the wolves wouldn't have it dug up this night, in any case?' Browne sat a little way off with his back to them, whetting a stone.

'Tell you what,' said Parmetar, 'if you two are good to continue on with this, I'll ride these containers down to the river. Should only be gone the half hour. You'll get finished up here, all right?' He wiped a bloody strand of hair from his forehead.

'Already begun,' said Browne. He stood up, scalpel in hand.

'Planning on take a dip out there?' said Jameson, looking at the blood-soused captain.

'I'll get in the water when I'm done,' Parmetar said, touching the lead mule with a light whip. 'Chah!' he shouted and river-bound, the wagon rumbled out.

X

SÉANCE: E.E. HENRY PHOTOGRAPHIC STUDIO, LEAVENWORTH

Familiar spirit: Junius Browne

BROWNE IMPROVISED A MORTUARY table, extending his show cart on one side beneath a tatty, raised canvas awning to make himself an outdoor operating booth. He lugged a whiskey cask from inside the cart, lowering it carefully to the ground, and then another and rolled them around the side and pulling them upright with some effort, hefted each into position. Having got a hold of a rear-quarter panel from the body of the busted mail-carriage, he sanded down one edge for splinters and rested it snugly on the hogsheads, creating a crude surgical table. Then he unrolled a bolt of linen so that the marginally convex carriage door table-top now looked laid with an altar cloth. He retrieved the body from its quiet resting place amongst squashes and hard-tack in the battered supplies wagon. Slitting the seed-sack shroud with a small penknife, he laid Edwards' cadaver on its back: its palms faced downward, its legs were straight and slightly apart. Edwards' corpse lay stiff and indifferent upon this rough operating table, its slim life once well-preserved by Clarke's own careful hands.

One by one, Browne filled the boy's eye sockets with rabbit glue and sealed them over, wiping sticky tears of residue that urged from beneath his delicate lids. He took cotton wads, ripped them and pushed the wadding into the boy's small mouth, padding out his thin cheeks. Then he threaded a long, curved, metal needle with well-waxed thread and sewed the mouth shut, knotting that thread just below the boy's bottom lip and, piercing the lower frenulum to pull the needle through the upper one, he drew it right up through the left nostril and across the boy's septum, then down the right hand nostril to pierce again both labial frenula and pushed the needle tip up into the nostril once more where he caught the loose ends of that waxy string and tied them and disguised the knot deep in the boy's nasal cartilage. Then he attempted to massage the boy's mouth into a smile, but his contracted lips were fixed and Browne waited before kneading more of the rigor mortis out of the stiffened muscles of the boy's morbid expression.

The embalmer now made his first incision, opening the boy's slim neck just along the collarbone with an inch-long scalpel cut. Locating the carotid artery, he prised it out with his aneurysm hook, slit it and inserted an arterial tube. This done, he made another nick, severing the jugular vein and inserted a cannula for the blood to drain off. Then he used a bulb syringe to push the embalming fluid through the boy's veins, heart, fingers and toes, clamped it and vigorously rubbed the corpse as if re-circulating a second life. Then he stood squeezing the embalming pump like a desperate and fast-panting lung. In less than two hours the first part was done. Flies clotted the metal bucket side-splashed with pints of blood.

Parmetar and Jameson came and stood for a while, looking on. They brought the embalmer some whisky-strengthened coffee, attempted to talk with him. But Browne's seclusion was obvious in his manner and his focus, in his abrupt movements and grunted responses, so that presently they left him alone.

He began the aspiration with a vacuum pump, after pushing the sharp end of a rusty trocar into the abdomen, aiming north-west for the boy's left ear to puncture his lungs and then perforated the heart and diaphragm, jabbing back and forth in a fan-shaped movement. He re-entered at a diagonal angle in alignment with the corpse's right ear and worked the carcass innards over again. Then he confronted the lower part of the abdomen, sucking out any feces and urine, punctured all the intestines so that they could fill with the fluid. He held a gravity bottle high in the air and flooded the channels with more preservative before plugging the dead boy's mouth and anus with a cotton gauze when the last of the liquids finally emerged. Now Browne pummeled at Edwards' small lips again until he puckered them into expression.

At last, fly-besotted and arms crossed, the boy smiled in his replenished skin like a recumbent saint. Fresh-looking veins blued his feet, criss-crossing his plumped limbs, but his darkened hair lifted in the wind like lightly-lifting strands of rotted silk. Browne combed through this childish hair, trimming it a little at the brow to create a fringe, then shaved the area around his head wound and cut it open a little, increasing its size and violence. The boy's hair was matted behind the ears like sheep-wool: as if grown for the lining of a nest, and Browne couldn't get the comb through it but decided not to shave the skull again, to leave this matting as a subtle contrast.

He took a little grease and slicked the boy's eyebrows with a toothbrush. Then he rubbed rose oil into the dried dermis of the corpse's hands and face and stained its lips and cheeks with a madder tint. He took a measure of velvet from a roll in the cart and cut out a little jacket, tacking round the seams and pinning it at the back so that it looked secure and disguised the neck wounds, but in truth, it was a hasty and ill-fitting costume.

The embalmer packed lavender and cloves in the coat armpits to counteract any stronger smells. 'Will have to touch him up in Loma,' he said to himself.

Then Browne took a few peacock feathers from his stock and a couple of dried strawflower heads, a wand of honesty and a tattered paper rose and fashioned them into a rough bouquet which he wired onto the boy's wrists, covering up this joining with the overlong jacket sleeves. Finally, he inscribed a small card which he then hung on a short piece of string around the boy's lifeless neck:

ROBERT MCGEE
AGE 9
KILLED BY SCALPING

He stepped back and after a moment's thought, wrote on the reverse side:

ROBERTO MCGEE
9 AÑOS
ASESINADO POR
EL CUERO CABELLUDO

A wake of turkey vultures now hopped on the scrubby ground, rasping with their roughened tongues, straining scrotal heads and chiding. One alighted on the blood bucket rim, sipping at its tangy slops. Browne shooed the vulture off with both hands outspread and the blood pail tipped over as the bird kicked it away in up-launched flight. Drawing his pistol, Browne fired a few rounds and the vultures moved upwards to a tree but flapped to the ground again as soon as his back was turned.

Then he worked fast, sawing up more of the carriage-wood and tacked it together to form an elongated diamond. He lifted the light body into it and then transformed the medical-table carriage panel (whose varnish had prevented it from in-soaking blood, preservative and all the other mortal fluids, except where the sanded part looked like a bank of browning coral) into a roughly-fitting lid. With the last of the tacks, he tamped the lid down and loaded the crude box into the back of the supplies wagon where it sat as if it had always been there, converting the small company of wagons into a funeral cortege.

First light turned to last light and within its brief compass the three men now worked over death, stamping at the twilight buzzards, burning off the patches of ground most badly steeped in blood. Eventually they corralled the wagons, watered the horses, roused and fed the remaining boy, then ate themselves, sitting silenced by fatigue round a campfire that softened with its flickering, their blood-flecked skin and blood-smeared clothing. It was done. The young corpse of Allen Edwards lay sightless and voiceless and bloodless, preserved in his makeshift, U.S. mail-carriage coffin.

XI

SÉANCE: E.E. HENRY PHOTOGRAPHIC STUDIO, LEAVENWORTH

Familiar spirit: Carlos de Lopez

A CRUSHED MARIGOLD TRAIL led us down to the banks of the Mora river. We plodded those pollen-fields whose flower dusts rose like the auriferous ash of a forgotten sacrifice: plowed that gold pollen as if plowing a dream-life of the dead. And in the sunlight stood a spirit, whose body billowed golden plumes of dust, recounting — as if to himself — the history of this place in his bearing and imagining both. Invisible to the others, I watched him walk beside us, the wide brim of his hat low on his forehead, the dagger sheath slim on his low-slung belt, silver rings high on his thumbs and forefingers, high near the knuckle joints, as he broke pan de muerto, pan de ánimas, broke bread and shared it out between the two of us, striding through his own stippled shadow of living and dying cempasúchiles, strolling those wild marigold fields on morbid stalks of the dead.

'I am local to here,' he said to me, and his voice was mild. 'My dance hall curtilage in Loma Parda extends right down to this river, to those lava caves that stud the soft, dark cliffs. Yes and my women still draw moans from soldiers who tremble like shaken bones in those caverns of the Cañon de las Pelones — Bald Women's Canyon, they call it. They say once a Captain Sykes captured a prostitute band. He rounded them up and shaved their louse-ridden heads. Their secret trade happened among mounds and mounds of plundered good hawked from the fat stores of Fort Union. Once, too, there was an old hermit who'd been ousted, spat at, beaten, He died muttering prayers in old Italian. His battered body was found by a slow turn in the river's bend and when the Lome villagers carried it back to mourn him, we found sugar supplies and coffee beans and sacks of dried peaches stashed in the rock face. The people considered these his bountiful offering. That was before my place, my *De Lopez Salon de Bailar, Casino and Cantina* flowered, yes floreció, around an adobe courtyard whose cribs I annexed for the use of pleasure. Now, those abandoned caves up there, hold only the phantoms of petroglyph makers and Navajo peaches, bordello girls and the dead pelones and — they say — the old wandering penitente's spirit. Nothing but a sign can purge them, yet no-one knows how to make its mark. Come, I will take you to the salon. You must know that tonight is part of a special festival. Tonight we wait for their spirits to come.'

A FAINT corrido rose on the river mist and I saw how the wagoners caught its cadence. In the encroaching dusk it was the song which led us: the wagon lanterns danced as our wheel felloes trammeled coarse ground. Soon we found the track had widened and hardened and the first Loma smallholdings appeared in the darkness and we slowed as the wheels grooved to the main trackway and crossing the heavy-planked bridge, came to the source of that sounded cantina as if coming to the very headspring of the Mora River.

Night fell into rough-scored dark, rilling with excitement. Above a light-splashed ground at the gate, faded paper ribbons trembled in transparent heat cast from two heavy, iron lanterns and the dull roar contained by the cantina mud walls seemed to give voice to the ghost of a crowd. The only prohibitive —

or perhaps protective, perhaps instinctive — thing standing between us and the salon was a red oak door pierced with a hundredfold glowing points, as if the sword tips of old matadors had pounced coruscating stellar maps across its worn surface.

'Whose those star charts were, I could not tell,' said the spirit to me, noting my interest, 'but they seemed to plot an embittered universe: Loma always spilled its bloods with ease, indifferent to overhead nocturnal warnings.'

Near the stone doorway a cat gnawed its wrist before bounding into deeper darkness as Jameson dismounted in the soft gloom and yanked the door's heavy bell-chain. Then he stepped back, listening.

'Y entonces,' rang a voice from the upper story, 'trae tus caballos por la espalda.'

So, quirting up the mules, we drove round the back of the place through the double doors of a livery archway dragged open before us. The empty courtyard within was uplit by sparse torches that shone patchily like fool's gold. Jumping down from the wagon box, the captain gave a low whistle.

'Mano estable,' he called and two stable boys came running through the darkness. They secured the gateway, unhitched the animals and led them off to water at the cantina stables. When the boys returned, the captain drew them over to Browne's vehicle and opened up the back of the cart. Large eyes ambered in the lantern light as the panther raised her upper lip, showing yellowed fangs. Both boys backed off, startled.

'No,' said the captain softly, squatting down to face them, tightly holding their small wrists. 'Ahora escúchame, es mansa pero no trates de tocarla, okay? No touching.' Then he stood up and tipped them a half-cent each and they scurried away, shadow-like.

'Oye,' he called after them, '¿Dónde está el jefe? Mi compañero quiere estar llevado con él.'

One of the boys paused, '¿Quieres ver de Lopez?'

'Si.'

'El Sr. Lopez no está aquí. Pero te llevaré a de Lopez.'

'Momento,' he said to the boys and turned to Jameson: 'How's McGee doing?'

'Sleeping.'

'Good for now, then.' He signed to the stable boys. 'We ought to get some food into him.'

'Let's fix up the show cart first. Shouldn't take long. She'll need feeding too,' Browne said as he bolted the wooden doors on the hissing cat.

Then the young boys returned wielding lanterns and pulled on the men's sleeves.

'Suavamente,' said the captain, brushing them off.

'Señor,' said one child, 'we take you to de Lopez.'

'Catalina! Catalina!' they cried, scampering ahead.

The captain laughed softly.

'What is it?' said Browne, picking dried mud off his coat.

'Catalina — she who bites. I'm intrigued to meet her.' Parmetar cocked his head, grinning.

The thin ghost of a woman emerged in a doorway. She was harassed and wore a flour-covered apron which she twisted and wrung in her hands as she spoke. There was the sweet smell of baked bread about her, but she was tired and handsome and without spare warmth.

'¿Qué deseas?' she said, drawing a strand of hair out of her eyes.

'¡Desaparecer!' she said to the small boys who disappeared,

wraith-like, into the dark.

'Señora, deseamos hablar con de Lopez,' said the captain, courteously.

Nodding her head, she held the door open: 'Sígueme.'

Her bustling step led us up a worn staircase. Half-way up, the newell cap came away in Jameson's fumbling hand and as he slotted it back, I saw it was damaged with age like a battle-scarred beast. We had paused for him on the landing of the second flight to catch us up. Catalina then slid the triple bar bolts across the surface of a small door and knocked lightly, as if knocking for a patient or a priest. There was silence. Looking us over, Catalina confided in me she had seen much worse.

'All that come here, are seeking something...' she said, mutteringly, 'though Fort Union has always banned illicit excursions.'

She showed me the fort's general perspiring into late night paperwork, a fly crawling across names of the condemned: Hookly, Neward, Pace. Sentenced to hard labor and lashings.

'Some lose a horse,' she said, 'some go absent without leave beyond the river's line of caves, some struggle back to face again the fort.'

And in a cyclical backdrop, I saw how the spirit women bled and birthed and harbored their diseases and drank and cried and sweated for the dime on oilskins and burlap under the black weight of field skies by night and cave ceilings by day.

'Once,' said Catalina, 'there was a cougar, mauled a whore and fled. Sometimes men perished too, in visiting.'

She pounded on the door again and then showed me more.

I watched as a corporal slipped, fell to his death in a dusty shower of clattering stones. Across the following few weeks, he decayed facedown on the leafy floor of the autumn ravine and became coyote fodder, buzzard feed.

Catalina leaned in now, whispering: 'She gathered his bones up in a wicker basket, Angelina de las Estaño-Estrellas, having picked her way down to the canyon bed and hoisted them up with her friend, Elisabeta's help on a rough, rope pulley to the ledge by the cave. Some said there had been 'amor verdadero' between them, Angelina and this dead corporal. 'Citas de amor en las hojas retorcidas'. . . love trysts in the twisted leaves. Others said she killed him, kept his bones beneath her bed. When de Lopez heard of the incident, he banned all excursions up to the caves. The loss of a soldier was a calculation readymade. A whore lost is dollar grave. Of course, Angelina in the end hanged herself.'

'And so,' she went on, 'the cribs were installed. A woman could wash herself out, keep a good supply of wicks and wax, arrange her trade in regular form, create a line in wait and deploy a colored shade; a red glow in the mud window signaling when she was free and not. De Lopez tried to control the peso and the dollar, but always a portion of tips was secretly hidden by the whores in crib crevices. They had to be inteligente, ¿no?

Some saved for a future that would never exist, though the dull metal coins seemed invoke it. Others used it for drink when the pain got bad. Sometimes wads stuffed in the crumbling walls were there with bats and owls for several decades. De Lopez kept a strong arm when the whole racket creaked with violence and his protected ones could retreat to the dancehall upper floor where his brother would sing and sign and forgive the women their collective sins and then it would start all over again. As if forgiven by death itself.'

Then she described how below, the salon seemed ambivalent to bloodshed. It was too early for fracas fever, she said. The men would be drinking slowly and blowing on their cards, and the girls — some wise, some lonely — would be wandering around in a careful colony, coming to rest on the soldiers' knees before rising again to serve mescal, champagne, beer. When they laughed, it was tinged just a little with tension, but entrapment helped them to relax, swaddled their fears. They knew the gap in the cage of their existence. The only way to truly escape.

'Si,' nodded the old woman, scratching dried scales of dough from her fingers, 'en la única forma.'

Often, it was under a full-blown moon: to the cliffs or caves with a bottle of pulque. Sometimes, in one of the cribs, late by night with a snuffed candle. Sometimes, out in the fields with a straight razor or stolen blade. To fall, to shoot, to cut: 'caer, disparar, cortar. . . sometimes, to imbibe poison. You will ask why they did not just leave but departing enacted an exact copy: once stained, always stained. Though,' she conceded, 'there were those who could marry but the fort turned them away as they went down to appeal, wanting to follow their men right down the trail.'

And so, the girls could choose to leave the cage of Loma life by a certain route whenever they pleased and this secret knowledge helped them. Even the soldiers were duty-bound to death. But the cherries had a concerted freedom, unless you counted the murdered among them:

+

MERCEDES, battered to death in the Cañon de las Pelones. The only complaint was that her rotted corpse had ruined the 4 grain sacks she was propped against. D. 1833: 19 YRS.

SOLERO, whose killer had filled
every dying orifice with semen;
her eyes gouged out and both
sockets sealed over with wax. D.
1847: 27 YRS.

SANSAFRA, The Little One, slit
open from chin to vulva. D. 1876:
AGE UNKNOWN.

ELISABETA, raped and killed by
soldiers whilst bearing a child and
abandoned in an arroyo.
D. 1860: 3o YRS

ANGELINA, suicided
by hanging on the
anniversary of
Elisabeta's death.
D. 1865: 18 YRS

+

CATHLEEN ALLYN, tortured
to death with a fer-de-lance. D.
1861: AGE UNKNOWN

+

CARINA, arms & legs
removed after being
bitten all over at intervals.
D. 1863: 51 YRS

+

CATALINA, ('myself,' she said
proudly) died of natural causes
D. 1883: 91 YRS

Why should these souls be known as wounded prostitutes above all else? As those who rode into dark under the cover of dark and offered damp flowers to the dark: these volatile *bailarinas de la muerte*, who had normalcy and courage and tenacity and humor, though death lingered in their skirts, hidden wild-gentle, sucking on the mud-soaked hems of the women like a child sucks on the corner of a blanket. Some enjoyed Loma life as a rich and loose fabric. Some, champagne-quipped, kept a ledger of desire. Not all was punitive. For some, this *danza de la sexualidad* kept the very bones of the buildings alive, grew the steady swell of cash and music, re-plastered mud walls not coolly indifferent to this architecture of the heart. Why should they not be known as the prima ballerinas of that vivid life, and so equally vivid death. They came to be known as *Los Peligros de Loma Parda* — the Loma Parda Perils — and after they had been interred for a while in the dust plots of the regional desert, other girls had the bones dug up and painted their skulls with wild flowers and character inscriptions, so that Catalina was covered in honeysuckle with DURA in scrolling letters inscribed on her frontal bone, and Carina became swathed in verbena and called FIEL, and Cathleen Allyn was daubed in violet-colored yarrow and named IMPERTINENTE; Angelina's pearls were crushed into a blue paste to depict iridescent gentians and recognized as VALENTE; Sansafra was named JUSTA and smothered in pimpernels and chamomile; Solero was decorated with Hookers onion flowers as HUMORÍSTICA; Mercedes, with rock jasmine and anemones was DELICADA.

The living girls labored to build a small adobe charnel house with white-washed walls and filled it with candles. In it, they placed the floral skulls atop their mounded skeletons and then made garlands dipped in wax of those flowers they had carefully painted onto bone, so that the ossuary interior was rustle-dry and delicate with scent: dog roses curling above those burnt, sugar-dark lacrimal bones, those blossomy craniums. With sable-tipped brushes and tubed pigments bought from a traveling peddler of powders, tinctures and paints, they applied crushed verdigris and copper pastes and varnished the flora in a heavy shellac, so that the skulls sat like fat shells, glistering in new coats of markings, fat shells the color of nicotine-stained walls papered with bouquets of flowering sea-grasses that flowed and bent, not in the breeze of a deep marine current, but in the moving sadnesses of the quiet prostitutes lonely at their mournful work. These, their wreathed offerings:

MERCEDES:
DELICADA
rock jasmine
anemones
D. 1833: 19 YRS.

SOLERO:
HUMORÍSTICA
hookers onion
D. 1847: 27 YRS.

SANSAFRA:
JUSTA
pimpernels
chamomile
D. 1876: AGE UNKNOWN

ANGELINA:
VALIENTE
blue gentians
D. 1865: 18 YRS

CATHLEEN ALLYN:
IMPERTINENTE
violet-coloured yarrow
D. 1863: 51 YRS

CARINA:
FIEL
verbena
D. 1861: AGE UNKNOWN

CATALINA:
DURA
honeysuckle
D. 1883: 91 YRS

The Biter — who had tortured Carina, had left his uneven tooth-marks on each of the other mutilated torsos, ringed a scarlet circle round his victims' nipples — was caught, court-marshaled, then released. Corporal Gibson returned one month later, on a verdict of inconclusive evidence. Then he disappeared and few, except the friends of the Peligros, recalled the infamous murdering soldier. And so, the men who were killers, killed both in and out of jurisdiction. The ones who had survived open campaigns and sieges, attacks and defenses. Indian killers, Confederate killers, Bushwhackers, Union killers, Jayhawkers, Women and Children killers. All passed through in some kind of uniform, all avoided the firm hand of the law.

'I have seen killers who are invisible: mostly men,' Catalina said, 'but not only. Some boys are good boys that come down here — young.'

She was interrupted by a sudden shout from within the room. 'Ah, he has woken. Un centavo,' she said and held out a floury palm.

Parmetar chafed his pocket and handed her a one cent piece.

She scrutinized the coin — bit it, and nodded: 'Entrar,' she said and pushed the door open, propping herself against its weight.

'Gracias,' said the captain as we stepped into the chamber, but she shrugged and turned, pulling the heavy door shut behind us that closed with a dull thud.

Then I heard the sliding shunt of each replaced bolt. My eyes strained to adjust to the dark. There was a sweetness of rust, of bark crushed in musk, its holy notes mixed with tobacco leaves. Bunched and dried vetch and cempasúchile hung from the overhead beams and the air was traced with pollen dissolved in blackness, out of which a cracked spirit voice, oracular — perhaps ventriloquised — now summoned its opening question: 'Catalina Alvina Chaireses bring you here?'

'Yes, sir,' the captain said, stepping forward now into the room.

The voice came again: 'She has not communicated with me for three years, no by word or sign. But she sends you, just as others she has offered to my loneliness. How may I be of use to you?'

'Could use a little light in here,' replied Parmetar, evenly.

'No es posible,' said the voice. There was a long pause. 'You gentlemen want to sit?'

'Gracias,' said Jameson. There was another pause as we remained standing.

'Momento.'

A single scratch bloomed a glow. Now, I saw the room stood empty bar a large, wooden confession box. Smoke gently seethed through its latticed panelling.

The captain coughed, and held a sleeve to his mouth.

'Entrar,' said the voice.

Parmetar whispered: 'This some kind of trick?'

'Pero, no. Come in, come in.'

Cautiously, we approached the polished box and inside, I dimly perceived a wooden bench.

'Bueno,' said the voice, as we took our seats.

In the vetch-mottled light, pungent with turning smoke, the voice began, as if in confession itself: 'Mi nombre es de Lopez. My people were here many generations. Survived the scourging of winters where snow burned into their sight. Storms and droughts that blew their crops away. They kept sheep in the river crevices and stored wine in las cuevas. Good wine. Then the fort came and the people were corrupted by soldiers. All take. None replenish.'

Smoke curled through the latticework as his voice ceased and then, as if inevitable after some time watching us, he asked: 'What is it that you wish to take?'

The embalmer spoke up: 'My name is Doctor Junius Browne,' he said, 'and I am a traveling man of medicine.'

'Un chamán.'

'Un curandero.'

'Un curandero,' de Lopez acquiesced.

'I have a boy with me, dead. Dead from sickness. I preserved him across many hours with a special fluid I made myself and now should like to show my work.'

'Acércate,' came de Lopez's voice.

Browne leaned forward.

'Acércate, acércate.'

So, kneeling now, Browne pressed his face to the grille. I saw what he saw — the detail of flesh: how de Lopez's stained ruff was loose about the neck, how his helmet shone dully in the flame, how the tincture of arnica was strong on him, how the cuirass sat on his naked form like a slightly-cracked crustacean shell, loosened off from sweat and muscle, how his features were bewildered by paint: red-daubed lips, red-daubed cheeks, and skin clarted white with the colors of the clown, as ash burred with glowing inhalation from his wet and slickened cigar nub, to fall on his steel bib like a seasonal dusting of snow, how his damp eyes watered above it all — this conquistador of the confessional.

In response to all this, Parmetar rose.

'No lo harás,' shouted de Lopez.

Browne, now laying a hand on Parmetar's arm, spoke in an urging acceleration: 'Señor, I have a confession. I have a confession to make.'

Silence fell. Slowly, the cigar smoke resumed its circulation.

'Mi confesión es esta: I killed the boy. I killed the boy and wish to display him as my penance. Your people here will pray for him and he will become once more living.'

De Lopez seemed to consider this, the glint of his breastplate betraying slight movement. 'Si,' he said at length, as the candle guttered. 'This box houses the most deepest fears within, is washed in atonement, my women remove themselves unburdened, refreshed by the antique star of a living lamb. Si,' sighed de Lopez. 'He — he, is my punishment. Wait, I show you,' he said, as the confession box flared into light from a relit wick. De Lopez now slid the grille to one side and sat in his armour, blinking at us. And in this flower-filled and smoke-beguiled place that seemed to conspire with dream against confession, he spoke as if from within a tinder-box, as if his very voicings could confer with flame and ignite the influx of some fundamental absolution. 'You ask me who I am,' he said. 'I am de Lopez. Estoy la muerte.'

And if, for a moment, the honeyed guise of laughter rose up in the men, it was quickly doused as the gargantuan raised a carafe and drank and passed it about. He paused, then — as if listening. 'Si, I am death,' he said. 'You, yes, you too — you are death. We are its definite knife points, arrowheads, ropes, horses, arsenic, age, gunpowder, extreme cold, extreme heat, the sicknesses of infants and of dogs, the killers of and deaths of beasts, water, fire, air, height, weight. . . we are all moving images of death. We are all mirrors broken to make such sharp weapons that prick death: so violent, so much ending, we must have horror to make death remember that death itself is us. You say I am death. I am death. One manifestation, here. You are death — all of you. But if tonight they tell you: "Ah, you were taken to see de Lopez, now you find death," this will be true also. "Oh, they keep death imprisoned in that room up there," this will be also true. You have come to visit me and now must be prepared. You must be strong to make death remember you as itself.'

Without taking his eyes from us, de Lopez raised the carafe high in the air, his naked arm shaking with its glassy weight. Then he deliberately let it slip and the bottle smashed on the floor. Among the smithereens: the glass shards and gashed black cherries, clove bits and slices of quince — he pounced on a glistening form like a snail or shucked oyster, and grasped it between two stained and corpulent fingers, and raised it to an open mouth, intook it, and closed that mouth and then resting with this small bit in his cheek, like a tobacco wad or hidden coin, said: 'I hold him in my mouth so he is safe. Like in the womb, no? In that glass bottle, I cannot hear him. They always put him back in again. But on my tongue he can sleep and I can hear him and he, yes he, can hear the inside of my words. Can hear me thinking, lying asleep in my cheek.'

He relit the dead cigar and drawing hard on the blackened nub, protractedly released its smoke. I saw his monolithic knees were badly cut. He sat for a moment, bleeding heavily, picking out splintered glass from his flesh. 'You can have your show for one night,' he said. 'Cincuenta, cincuenta. You come to me here at nine tomorrow morning.'

'Entiendo,' said Browne, scuffling onto the hard bench behind him. 'Entiendo.'

De Lopez seemed pleased and in one last gesture of intent pursed his lips, raising his helmeted head, and the small fetus began to emerge like a mucosal tongue. He paused, as if under tremendous strain. Then he in-sucked it again and slid back the grate.

'Cosmo,' came a clear voice from the entrance to the room, as light was thrown across us.

De Lopez released a long howl: 'Mi hijo,' he wailed, 'mi hijo.'

We emerged rapidly then from the cramped interior of the confession box, blinking.

'You have been in here long?' said the spirit, and I recognised him from our arrival in the pollen fields.

'Some time,' said Browne.

'Forgive him, my brother. He is not at all right since the death of his son. We try to keep him apart — who let you in?'

Browne gestured vaguely.

'I see,' said the spirit of the man, as he ushered us toward the door. 'I will speak with her later. My name is Carlos de Lopez, I am the owner of the *De Lopez Salon de Bailar, Cantina and Casino*. Please, let us go for some refreshments and you can tell me how I may be of help.'

He opened the door, waited and closed it hard behind us, bolting it securely again. 'Please,' he said.

We followed his swift descent down the staircase out into the swelling music of the cantina courtyard.

'Tres mezcales,' he called to the attendant barman. 'No — una botella,' he corrected himself. 'Please —' he indicated to a small table and when we were seated, served out four short glasses himself. Over agave, Browne began his proposition afresh.

When he had finished, de Lopez said: 'You came down the crossing alone? No escort?'

'Si,' said the captain.

And you brought with you a dead boy, a preserved boy. Un niño momificado?'

'We did,' said Browne.

De Lopez fell silent for some time. 'This is an exceptional night, not a night for provoking the dead, but of deep friendship and celebration with them: a night of prayer, food, tenderness for their spirits. We don't weep for our dead in case we make their route back to the afterlife wet with our tears, slippery and dangerous. Tomorrow we go up to the gravesite to decorate the burial ground with marigold petals. Your show might not be so out of place this evening. My brother drives a soft bargain,' said de Lopez, gazing out across the plaza. 'For death, he drives a soft bargain. Okay by you, if we make it sixty-forty?'

Browne finished his shot. 'Okay by me.'

'Good. You can bring it to me in the morning. I will,' he said, 'be busy tonight.' He got up. 'This used to be a good place, before Fort Union. Many families were here, good families. Now we have this —' In one slow-encompassing sweep he gestured from left to right across the outcrop of buildings. He looked as if making an incomplete sign of the cross. Browne also stood up, but this thing de Lopez conveyed seemingly meant little to him.

'You got mighty good mezcal,' was all he said in response.

'Un secreto,' replied de Lopez with a slight click of his heels, but his eyes had already dimmed in the knowledge that such intimations fell on hard ground and I sensed he knew a little less of the strangers, and a little more of himself as the darkness further enveloped us all.

'Aquí no hay historia, he said to himself, 'aquí hay una oración. Pero nunca será respondido y ese es su milagro integral. Buenas noches,' he called as he strode into the courtyard, one arm upraised high in the cold night air, as if in casual half-surrender.

XII

SÉANCE: E.E. HENRY PHOTOGRAPHIC STUDIO, LEAVENWORTH

Familiar spirit: Junius Browne

'WHAT YOU WILL WANT to know,' said the embalmer's ghost, speaking bluntly to me now, as the saddle-naked horses stood quiet in their stalls, 'is whether I have thought to preserve a human soul. And so knowing, if I could cure yours also — your ghost, enigma, phantasm — as long ago in England, in those secretive experiments of roses and ash, when a shrub could be raised from the dead and kept in a glass. Harvey took a dove's heart, trilling on his thumb, and made reckonings of the blood's beat, its watch, its timing. I have not yet done one thing of worth, but that river crash brokered a new season. My splintered cart led to more than a bonfire: it was a sign of change, a roaring conflagration chocked with symbols of my own advancement.'

Browne sighed and continued on in a low voice that filled the stable's dimness: 'You have heard of beheaded conquistadors, spiked on a frame with the heads of their horses. Rolled in the dusts of time, those horses. Perhaps their equine spirits are still around us. . . I should need to know the hook, the exact mode, the implement to draw them down. That is all it is: an opening, a process. As in the labyrinth's quixotic trail — sometimes to me it seems we ride endless packs of bulls, that the flocks of wild buffalo are minotaur flocks, that the thread is the endless western trail that, though straight, has bewilderment that remains in the head: an amazement. Well, my friend, the trick with the labyrinth is always to know whether you moved to go in or moved to come out: knowing this, you won't get lost.'

He paused as sudden lamplight cut the floor and a figure came with a bucket of water. The embalmer tipped him, watched him leave, then rolled up his shirt-sleeves in expert movements, loosening his chemise a little at the neck, untucking its hem from his dingy trouser-band and then bent from the waist to wash in the bucket, still half-sitting on a straw bale, lifted his shirt up and over the back of his head without entirely taking it off, and I saw his torso was a wickerwork of scars.

The sound of water wetted the silence as steam rose and he sighed again from the wash-cloth's heat. Then he sat a long while, dripping, sat unmoving as if entranced, as if in a coda of his dream. 'I have a brittle head for stars,' he said to me at length, as the horses snorted, hushed in their stalls. 'Perhaps that's why they escape me. What a palimpsest of death the night sky is.' He got up, pulling at his damp chemise to tuck it in again at the belt and uncorked a flagon. 'All will say how good it is, yet none will replace their whiskey with water. I am piloting the destiny of two small souls: a binary destiny — one living, one dead. Choose your whiskey, choose your water. Almost grafted together through injury, I shall exploit their experience and reduce it to ash.'

He now wandered about in the still-listening dark, coming to rest his heavy arm on a young roan stallion. 'I put my ear to his flank,' Browne said, 'hope to hear the pulse of his heart.' He turned now, rolling to lean back against the horse that stepped lightly in discomfort, back and forth, and whisked its tail drily in the gloom.

'Roses and ash wash over him,' said Browne, 'roses and ash rinse off his sin.'

He lolled there a moment longer and then slowly stood upright.

'And you,' he addressed the panther, 'is it that you've lost your scream?'

He kicked the wooden box and the large cat snarled and turned restlessly. Her aurous eyes seemed to absorb the darkness, to burn it up as an illuminate fuel and exude it in solar intensiveness. I could not look at her for long, shackled in a cage, but inhaled the feline tang and knew she smelled me too, lunging impotently on her tether, among the honeyed straw bales, the musk of the horses.

Browne nudged the kickover bolt on the stable door to push it open and fresh air flooded the stone-walled interior, an air flecked with flame-light and voices.

'Look at the stands,' he said, 'look at the breads and the flowers. They say the spirits come in to feast and when they leave the food has a different taste, is lighter too, in weight.' He turned back toward the stable darkness and it seemed to me his eyes glowed like the panther's. 'If I can resurrect palingenesis itself, if I can grow the boy from a body of ashes — from his own incinerate form — there would be no need for all this,' he gestured at the courtyard prayerful. ' You could keep the spirit strong in a smaller, but vigorous form.'

He addressed the horses like a political orator, as they whisked off flies, irreverent and mute. Then Browne lit a lantern and shadows were thrown right up onto the high stone walls and the stable became a momentary theater of erratic paper puppet movements. There were sounds of quickened preparation and silhouette motion within the wagon: Browne, a shadow man, lifting tools. The awnings were pinned back. A box dragged and lifted and placed. The light re-positioned. Browne shuffled in the semi-dark, clearing his throat, and cursed beneath his breath now and again with exertion. The horses stood without moving, without brushing the flies from sweaty flanks and the oil lamp burned with a steadily uprising flame, drawn longer than a flame should have been, as the glass walls of the lantern blackened. Then someone moved as shadow in the straw bales by the stable door.

'Jameson,' said Browne, dropping down from the wagon.

'Came to lend a hand.'

'Not much now left to do. Parmetar with you?'

'Nope. He's gone lady hunting.' Jameson spat expertly on the flagstones. 'Heard some of your plans just then. Sounded a little profligate.' He jerked his thumb at the wagon. 'He still asleep?'

'Asleep as he'll ever be,' said Browne bending to pick up the water-flagon. He let the liquid flow a little down his chin and neck. 'Want some?' he said.

'How much you given him?'

'I'll wake him in a bit. He needs food. Boys are like butterflies: need sugar and water and opium and will survive just fine.'

Jameson wandered around the stable. 'Don't like your plans, Browne. We need to get that boy healed up. Should take him on over to the fort in the morning.'

'Morning's all set, got another play to put on.'

'All right,' said Jameson, 'afterward, then.' He turned back to the embalmer and faced him.

'Come on with me and we'll make some dollar on them. Take them north, it's a better circuit.' Browne recapped the water bottle and propped it on the wagon box.

'I don't like it. Not one bit,' said Jameson. 'You get this thing

done and make your money and then I'm taking the kid down to the fort. You can keep the other one. Parmetar's gone bad and now you are on the edge of something. It ain't right,' said Jameson. 'It just ain't right.'

A quietness now fell between them. Then Browne came in close to the other man

'Ever come across a cut of rotted meat,' he said, 'and found yourself both hungered and revulsed by the stench?'

Jameson shrugged.

'Well that's what a pit show is. You can have all the fools from the beginning of time patting out the dance of death: then make them stand still in wood, in stone, but it is all still alive in the bone. That boy in there is a living dance of death and the skeleton of the great slayer himself demands to me he dance it out.'

XIII

SÉANCE: E.E. HENRY PHOTOGRAPHIC STUDIO, LEAVENWORTH

Familiar spirit: Angelina de Las Estaño-Estrellas

HIGH IN THE SPIRIT salon, de Lopez's sign was thick cigar smoke wreathing torn paper lanterns strung along the dancehall walls, circling translucent vases of cempasúchiles placed upon the dozens of trestle tables spread with dust-darned cloths and upon those, water jugs and glasses and bottles of reposado sotol and flagons of colonche and clay pots for ash and spittoons and playing cards and dominoes and beyond those, across that sea of crowded tables, was an intimate stage, a crude platform of layered planks, and on it performed a band, barely discernible above the roar, barely visible through the smoke. This skeletal, in-house quintet comprised only a vihuela player, a guitarrón player, one small boy trumpeter, a Spanish guitarist and an old fiddler. Sometimes they nervously made a circuit, to play their instruments at the patrons' tables, their music moving through human voices. At other times, if things got rough, they retreated to their tiny stage and sang slow-lilting ballads at the mob. When glass took to air, the players withdrew, peering from behind a ragged curtain. They lit black cigars, drank large pulques, and patiently observed the raucous vision.

'A bullfight with too many bulls. Then again,' mused Carlos de Lopez to his young companion, 'too many toréros. Whichever way you look at it, blood flows in song and song flows in blood.'

Within the uproar, Parmetar stood for a while at the double swing-door, then at de Lopez's sign, made his way over to his table, found a broken chair and sat down.

'Angelina,' said de Lopez, speaking in a loud English, 'meet our new visitor. Perhaps you can entertain him. . . entretenerlo.'

The young girl seated at the table surveyed Parmetar solemnly as de Lopez took his leave and made his way over to the bar, conferring with the young men serving there.

Parmetar watched him and then, turning his attention back to the young woman, patted the chair right next to him.

Tentatively, Angelina accepted his invitation, getting up to move across. She was a small spirit with high hips, a slight waistline and possessed long and lightly furzed legs. That night she was costumed in turkey-feather wings and carried a field worker's hand-scythe and had a skull-painted face so that the whole of her bearing became one of an incongruous ángel de la muerte. She had a smear of red on her burnt lips and a red daub on each ashen cheek and her jet hair was oiled in an interlaced plait that hung in a sinuous whip down the length of her spine. To cover the rope-burn around her neck she wore a set of pearls once stolen for her from the Fort Union safe which she had always considered her potential dowry. In hair carefully arranged over her left ear, a bronze marigold wilted and every so often would fall to the ground and distractedly she would lean down to pick it up, all the while surveying the room.

'Remind me of your name?' Parmetar said.

She stared at him blankly.

'¿Cómo te llamas?'

'Angelina de Las Estaño-Estrellas.'

'¿Qué?'

She leaned in closer, shouting in his ear.

Angel of the tin star. That's quite a name.' He lit a cheroot

143

and sucked on it meditatively, keenly surveying the crowded cantina. 'A poor soldier's tied up in the sun or the rain, with a gag in his mouth till he's tortured with pain,' sang Parmetar under his breath. 'Si —' he raised a finger to the attendant mesera, who came and measured out a drink and waited while the captain downed it, listless for the dollar and the change. Parmetar sang hoarsely: 'Why, I'm blest! If the eagle we wear on our flag, in its claws shouldn't carry a buck and a gag.'

The mesera eyed him, slowly shaking his head.

'Otro,' motioned Parmetar and while it was served, adjusted the dirt-tight seam at his belt and licked a forefinger and thumb, fiddling his mustache ends into points, and straightened his coat and belted holster, and: 'Here, lend me a comb,' he commanded a passing soldier, who reached down into his boot and gave him one. The man was fair and young with the desert stamped all over his eyes.

'To have and to hold,' said the captain, returning the hair comb.

The soldier gave a vague salute and stumbled through the broken-down swing doors.

Parmetar turned to the girl: 'What you want to do, you want to go?'

'Si,' but she didn't move and lolled on her chair, dull with exhaustion, looking like a death's head moth.

They had a corner set-up where the high plaster wall above them was a peeling turquoise, hung with bright paper flags and a marigold-festooned madonna stood blindly in a flickering alcove filled with melting beeswax stems that dripped down the lower portion of the wall in fragrant yellow stalactites.

'Want another?'

'Si quiere,' she shrugged. The flor de la muerte tucked behind her ear slipped forward, dangled for a moment, and landed limply on the table.

Lifting it between his finger and thumb, Parmetar rotated the blossom by the stem, twirling it back and forwards. '*No* —' she said, as he leaned in toward her, thinking to fix it back in her hair, but was startled to find the girl's ear lightly covered in a soft black fur. He adjusted the small floral trophy without saying a word and Angelina torpidly watched him do it. The captain sat back and relit the cheroot.

'You don't much go in for conversation, do you?'

She looked at him.

'Entiendes inglés?'

She demurred, tracing the blunt blade of her scythe.

'Bueno,' he refilled his glass. 'Bueno. Guess your age might be very young.'

'Creo que estas asustado,' she offered, barely audible.

'Asustado — you think I'm scared, do you? Por qué?'

She shrugged.

'A stock line, is what I think.' He rubbed her plait end between finger and thumb.

'¿Qué?'

'Something you tell all the boys.'

'No.'

'Well, just maybe I do have something to be frightened about. You might be right there.'

¿Por qué?' Angelina flung her plait over one shoulder, and pulled the rough little woolen shawl she was wearing tighter around her, and rested both elbows on the rickety table, cupping her chin in small hands.

He looked at her: 'You don't ask for much, do you. All right,' he said, retrieving a card from the inside of his coat. 'Seen this girl? ¿Has visto está chica?'

In a swift, childlike gesture she felt for the fingers of his hand and held them briefly in her own as she took the faded carte-de-visite of a woman.

Listlessly she looked over its image and passed it back to him, saying: '¿Quieres ir?'

THEY SLIPPED out then, and found an empty crib and afterward lay nakedly in the dark where he confided in her like a sister or sweetheart, as gently she stroked his gaunt-boned face. The darkness hid them from each other and his confession filled that darkness like a dead hope.

'It was a long crossing,' he began, settling back on the cot. 'I was sent out with three wagons, twelve mules. There was myself and three others, military soldiers, sent on down with me to Fort Union from Fort Larned. Know where that is?'

She said nothing, caressing his head.

He carried on regardless: 'East of here,' he said. 'We had a deal of ground to cover,' he said, 'un largo viaje. I had a clear aim on coming here, right over to Loma Parda. Didn't much fancy my prospects at Union. But we had strange cargo. Had a couple of boys with us, badly hurt. That fairly complicated things.'

Angelina's gaze wavered imperceptibly.

'We forged McNee's Crossing from the Point of Rocks, and the Rock Crossing of the Canadian River, and Wagon Mound; forded Coon Creek and Mulberry Creek and Sand Creek; traversed Rabbit Ears Creek, Rock Creek and Whetstone Creek, and then we passed through La Junta with its thick, squat dwellings. Overcame ruts, shingles and washes that criss-crossed the Kansas and New Mexico trails. We'd not paused but moved secretly, without a parade. Had bypassed the jump-off point at La Junta and so timed the trail for isolated journeying. Came in alone. We'd already done a fair bit and were fair worn out.' He relit his dead cigar, shaking out the fiery match head, then lay again on her warm arm. 'Was a fierce thunderstorm one night.' He paused to inhale. 'The eye of a crow would have scanned the air and seen five figures prostrate on the ground, lying well away from the stationary wagons. Finger-length whips of crackling light inched closer to us minute by minute and we were pounced hard by hail. When we stood up again, we were wild figures of mud, our open canteens were refilled with storm water whose surfaces bobbed with bullets of ice. Couldn't get a fire going for a clear day after. Kindling was soaked, sagebrush was soaked, so we took one of the hay-filled sacks from beneath the wounded boy and tipped kerosene onto it and it lit for a short time in a roar-burning bush — groped for some tumbleweed root to keep alive this small conflagration. The fire consumed a shirt and a blanket, and so we now fed in turn on warmed beans and griddled bacon and sat by the dwindling blaze trying to thaw out our thunder-logged bones. That was on the thirteenth day and passing,' he said. 'We were grizzled and rain-soaked, mud-dried and footsore, but we kept warm, which was all that mattered.'

Parmetar took another drag and drew Angelina to him. Squaring her up in the dimness, he scrutinized her, then continued: 'What am I talking about. . . I'm down here, having got out. Was up for hanging,' he said. 'They always wanted me out. Had an overseeing at the Fort, was a pretty good captain until that surgeon came and I was damned if any letter farming me out, for fruit farming or whatever kind of farming, was going to reach the ears of Curtis. So I intercepted him. Took a bit of glass and slit his throat.' He paused there, gauging her reaction. 'Trouble was, they found him. Should've pushed him off that ravine, know I should. Thing is, I had to get down here. If I could only get close. Needed to get them to send me to Fort Union, then I'd be close to this godforsaken place. I can tell you I was a whole world dead inside and you would have to take my word for it. I can tell you that I break spirit with a spirit and that spirit is not my own. That spirit is Elizabeth's.'

The captain shifted his weight on the cot and then rolled onto his back, one hand cradling his head. He lay gazing upward. His liquor-seared mind seemed trapped in the telling of the tale. Angelina rested her head on his thin-boned chest and she played with the dead marigold.

'You ain't registering a thing I say,' he tested. Slowly, she dragged a petal over his sternum.

Parmetar settled down again, every word an unburdening: 'So that's how they got me in the end. Only, I got them. Was dying in that fort anyway. Sent me on down to Union under escort but we had a couple of boys with us, real hurt. One of them died. . . I recall that morning had a bloody-red dawn and I know it because I was woken by one boy, standing like a wraith over me. When I went with him to check the ambulance, one of them lay dead. That was after we rescued the wagon. Met a doctor out there on the trail. Well, I made a good suggestion which was that we disburse ourselves of both boys, alive and dead, by handing them over to the doctor. Spoke about his ability to embalm the night before, around the fire. He also said he was headed down here. There was a fracas. Some agreed with me about coming on down here, but two men wouldn't hear of it. . . well, some didn't survive that. Perhaps,' he paused, 'well, that soldier-nurse was regrettable. The one seeing to the boys. Could have done with her around. Seems there was just the doctor and me standing at the end. He collected my paperwork from the inner lining of one soldier's coat. I stripped those two soldiers of their uniforms and I burned those and my colleague set to fixing up the dead boy, then. Took him a little over four hours. I was near sick at the sight of it all. Couldn't forget the boy's open neck, the blood glinting in the tube.'

Angelina gazed up at him, unmoving.

There was silence in the crib and the air felt close.

Parmetar rolled into a sitting position and rubbed his neck. 'So you see why I may be a little frightened,' he said. 'Got the show being set up now. Browne's out there getting it done. Don't know that we should be here at all. Place is riddled with soldiers. Still, I don't need no reason for speaking with you, seeing as you seem nice and all.' He pushed Angelina aside and stood up, reaching for his clothes.

'¿Estás segura que no has visto esta chica? This is real important now. You sure you never seen this girl?'

Angelina shook her head, looking properly again, but then her eyes darkened.

'Elizabeth. Lizzie Parmetar?' He questioned hopefully, desperation flooding his voice.

She shook her head, but I saw she was trembling.

His face, then — his whole being — seemed to fade. 'Guess not,' he said and relit the cigar. 'Guess that was some long time ago now, hoped she might still have been out here. Someone wrote and sent me this picture card. I had a mind to come out here and find her. Needed to see if I could find her. She had una quemadura,' he said softly, tracing the line of Angelina's face, 'disfigured her entire left eye. A livid burn. It ran from forehead to chin, and she was scorched round the temple. Her beautiful hair. Wouldn't grow there again.' He paused and sucked on his cigar nub again. 'I did that to her,' he said.

The lamplight flickered across Angelina's face.

'Well,' he said with a hardness in his voice, 'guess she ain't here.' He took the photograph and tucked it away again.

'¿Cuánto?' he said, retrieving a thin roll of dollar bills from his pants. There was a pause. '¿Cuánto te debo?'

'Nada,' she replied, smiling at him.

'Go on, take it,' he said, seeming wary of a sudden attachment.

She shrugged and accepted the bills without counting them.

Then he saw it. 'You're no cherry,' he said.

She looked at him quizzically. '¿Qué?'

'Una cereza. . . talonadora,' he hesitated. 'Una puta?'

'No,' she said, false surprise in her young voice. '¿Por qué?'

'I thought,' he faltered. 'What are you doing here?'

She sat up, sucking her hand. 'Soy sobrina de Carlos de Lopez.'

Parmetar grasped her by both shoulders.

'Si and I speak good American,' she said gently and smiled.

He struck her hard then, across the face. She fell back onto the soiled blanket. He hit her again: Angelina de Estaño-Estrellas, named for a base-metal, eaten up by her own star whose sign did not favour her. Beneath the bed, the stashed bones of Corporal Gibson shunted with each calculated blow. Presently, Parmetar stopped. Blood festooned the oily pillow but, when he shakily lit the only candle, it apparently shrank to nothingness: Angelina balled up on the coverlet, arms wrapped tightly around her head, lay unconscious.

Must find the others, he thought urgently — *time to go.*

Parmetar gathered his things fast, but as he turned away, her sickle blade — glinting in the darkness — twisted in his ribs.

He crumpled sideways.

Angelina wiped the dull scythe on Parmetar's shirt sleeve, and rifling through his dirty clothes, found the cabinet card. Elisabeta. She kissed its worn surface. After Elisabeta was killed by Gibson's men, Angelina always swore at night —recalling how they had lain in the darkness, sleepily holding one another's hands — that she would avenge her friend twice by destroying the man who had slaughtered Elisabeta, and again the one who had burned the face of her friend. She cannot understand what she has done to be so fortunate that Elisabeta's tormentor might be brought directly to her; needed only to stab him once for the picture's proof.

Angelina left the crib door latched from the outside and in the cool evening courtyard, carefully relit the captain's salty cigar nub. The night sky was only punctured by stars, as if the moon had shrunken back with dread, but she turned Elisabeta's card in the match-light, peering at its reverse. *Elizabeth Mary Parmetar, 18*— the handwriting said, and Angelina read it again, trembling violently in her considered revenge. Then she abandoned James Parmetar's body in the darkness of the crib, left Elisabeta's brother there, like a sound trapped within a room.

XIV

SÉANCE: E.E. HENRY PHOTOGRAPHIC STUDIO, LEAVENWORTH

Familiar spirit: James Parmetar

AND THE FIRST MEN were fruit men, James Parmetar's people. Nurtured all that he had riled against, harboring orchard lands and schemes of apple-grafting; powder and liquid concoctions for treatments against canker, wood rot, flies and worms.

Now, the captain's spirit showed me how once he had been a young apple hunter in those fruit plains of Woodson county. Mother, father both dead then. Honored by grasses. Flesh peeled and cored to reveal an inner hysteria of insects. Heart beating tears then ceased. Drier then - and learning to read. Sunlight waxed and waned in those sugared grasses, moved temperature's time. He had watched. Eyelashes bristled with the salt of sleep. Listened. His small thumb pushed into a decayed planet, pippins thudding to earth around him, grazed the sun mist. Apples court death. He stood and threw his shadow off. I could hear Mr Baird, their spirit guardian, calling.

Cessation of leaf, cessation of thunder. Scented air that tasted of lightning. The apples hung lower, heads bowed for onslaught. Trees shivered and the horizon tightened in a hairline fracture. He who stumbles, stuns. He pelted for the homestead, plunging through thick wet fruit trees blurred to a damp gold. A coyote carcass rotted in its black pool of blood. The creek thinned there, plumed in dust that received rain in studded blows. The first drop hit the back of the boy's neck bullet-cold. Later he would come to know a bullet's scorch. Now he pelted warm-wild and glad of the jagged shape of the house that lifted and fell in time to his panting. Half-skidded down to the peeled and fraying front steps. The dog sheltered beneath, blood-old eyes peering out of a darkness the smallholding kept at its own feet. Baird at the door frame stood with linens and hot water.

'Oh no,' the boy shouted, 'am I sick?'

A cacophony of giggles. Baird's face, a grimace of mirth. Large handed, he tickled James, then clutched him fierce. The fire was lit. Baird toweled the boy's rough head like a pup, rubbed back to life. Ears ringing. Now for soup and hot apple. Yes. Thunder rumbled overhead. Lightning flickered, snake-tongued, and the whole room blenched fractionally, then returned to fire gloom.

'Got your lesson done?' said Baird.

The boy nodded.

'To bed now, James Parmetar. Elizabeth and Laura have already settled down.'

It was done. The boy dreamt. Now wild woodpeckers called him from sleep. And the wind worried through wet fruit trees as if the hand of time rearranged their tattered leaves.

I looked on, watching their old guardian.

'He is stalked by a demon,' Baird muttered to me, pushing at the fire with a rusted iron. 'That orchard killed his parents. Unmerciful. This no Eden, it slayed them both in their prime.' And his gnarled hand increased its grip on the fire poker's twisted work.

All about the room shadows wrestled and Baird slept, witless — his own shade a low hill line, a soft shape on which the shadow forms flickered and thralled. In his eightieth year he was by then aged. Did not trouble, except for the children. They shall inherit the garden, Baird knew, signing the paperwork in a fierce hand. Shall inherit the fruits of this earth.

'Catastrophe struck in the youngest of us — in my sister, a girl of four: Laura she was called,' the spirit of Parmetar said to me. He lit a fresh cigar. 'Was tangle-haired and wood wild. Sucked her thumb to sleep and was somewhat scared of the wind. Pneumonia laid her down to rest. When a passing man came by, I remember how Baird ushered him in and he watched on, wild-eyed. There was a strong stench from the man, he had long brown fingers and spoke strange words, hunched over the white wax face of my littlest sister. He murmured prayers and ate hard. This was in the old parlor, and upstairs Elizabeth waited — childish now, pettish now — at thirteen. Bickered constantly with me: the year before we had quarreled and I pushed her and she fell into the fire. The burn healed well, but left a scar and she changed after that, was sullen and depressed-seeming.'

Now James revealed how that afternoon, when the gray-dark air was drizzled with flame-light, she had waited upstairs before slipping down to listen in — overheard the conversation with Baird and this strange stranger, that he was headed out west, that he had a cart outside.

'By suppertime we found she had gone, and though Baird rode on out that instant after the man, it was as if he had vanished — had never been and never gone. Baird launched a full-scale hunt which yielded nothing. Took advertisements out in all the county papers. Went out himself on forays into nearby places of isolation. After months of enquiries she never was found.'

I saw how that summer, old man Baird died and his passing was marked on one wall of the bedroom with a single blood-printed impression and his sheets were scrawled with urine, and prayers for him seemed to settle somewhat about the ceiling. The pastor called and then was gone. Only one candle flame licked over Baird's stiff corpse. Then a fever began in James, his eyes crabbed in the dim light.

'For three nights I dreamt of the dappled orchards, fruit flies thronging at my feet,' he said. 'Then those bad Kansas storms came in.'

He showed me fruit trees grown abrased and blackened in their sumps as merciless weather launched at the earth. Rough-cut letters he had scored into tree bark now became threatened as wild fires coursed the county in a criss-cross of flame. One morning he woke to find the homestead struck by lightning, the barrels burning with an acrid smell of scorched fruit. Ten hours later and the neighbors hadn't been able to put the fire out.

'Seemed there was nothing left to salvage,' he said. 'So I took off.'

I watched the ghost of the boy James as he scuttled the south orchard through fruit trees and squat beehives that sat like blanched pagodas fizzing in the heat-struck air, watched him run on beyond the paddock. The rotted apples he stood on had imploded into estranged shapes: weird legions, underworld battalions of death. Behind him the house was a licking column of smoke, spattered with dismal flame and the boy ran on into a future that would emphatically regain this, his past, among the putas and dried bones, the whiskey and marigolds. This was the fire's orchard dream.

XV

SÉANCE: E.E. HENRY PHOTOGRAPHIC STUDIO, LEAVENWORTH

Familiar spirit: Robert McGee

ABRUPTLY AND QUITE VIVIDLY, a young spirit came and stood beside me (as if mediated by a moribund sheerness: a vivacity made fainter by a once-sheer proximity to death: or a once-lived sheerness, in which anything dense was made slightly the less so, as if enforcedly made translucent by an act of passing existence — like vellum stretched across a small drum, or a paper-thin flower's desiccate skin, or a window sheathed with young ice melting). Yes, he came and he stood right beside me and there was a translucence to his vivid face.

And to say his eyes were like the shadows of a large room into which many ghosts crowdedly teemed, would be to say his eyes were occupied... though I wasn't quite certain... they seemed to capture a vast expansion of human vacuity, laced with an abrupt and quite vivid pain, as if his personality was of the eyes alone — and so one of only a 'sheer' or 'not-altogether' presence or person — then infilled by the hue of mere phantom. His eyes then, the undistilled color of cloudy water, were spectrally suffused, were spirit-toned.

His name was Robert, he said.

And I strained to hear that small, numbed voice.

'But they call me Bobby.'

Yes, he'd been young for a drover, as Crowe had said, yet somehow he seemed to have gotten even younger. How he'd done that, I didn't know, but it was despite those hard-aged eyes

— part-sagacious, part-pinched of love — as if he'd found a core stratum of himself: hit a preternatural seam of self-compassion.

He clambered down from the wagon bed and stood cautious in the empty stable, blinking in the half-light. That straw-colored hair of his I'd seen way back down the trail, now looked ashen and those equally ashen eyes, irradiated keen sorrow. This was the first entity I'd met to emanate any kind of light (normally kept so close to the spirit heart, I thought), but the boy shone softly as if his blood ran phosphorescent in a glow-worm luciferin that illumined his veins, that gave even the air around his movements light-seared wavelengths. At times, it was as if our spirits were touching. At times — though not-alive, he gave a better light to gesture, thought, instinct.

'Got a show tonight, Bobby?'

He nodded, a halo trembling round his head.

'You afraid?'

'I want to go with the other kids.'

He gazed at me then and slipped across to the stable door. Then he turned, hovering. His clothes, raggedly luminescent, had a fetor about them, strong as a set of heraldic colors, or bright rosettes, and I realized he'd been given Edwards' old duds, saturated with the stains of death.

'On you go, then,' I said.

He pushed open the stable door with a gaunt hand, went out to roam the courtyard. After him, a rush of light-enfolded atmosphere turned like scintillated smoke or thickened reverse-shade — *ah yes, that was it*, I thought, as if he cast a luster instead of a shadow.

Outside, the warm evening air teemed with the spirits of wandering children, smelled of sugar and bread and molten wax, and fruit and dried flowers, and prayer-scented ash. I'd never seen so many young ghosts, milling across the ground, carrying carved wooden toys, and small stitched dolls, and tottering sometimes, and bawling, if very young or overtired, and ambling slowly with that deep, childish concentration among the tiered courtyard stalls to select and examine sugared things: the kid, the lamb, the faun: wild sugar forms suckled on heat that could be bought for a coin and was theirs to keep close.

This, a picture for the faltering heart.

The boy melted away among them and for a while I tracked his luminous presence, but at last the childish throng obscured him and instead I watched the slow-moving villagers, mostly women with their dark heads covered, wearing parti-colored, striped rebozos, here and there taking a slim, brown wrist to lead a child up to the rural graveyard, carrying copperish oranges and pan de muerto baskets, fruit tenates, reed chiquihuites and petates to sit upon, donned in rustily-flickering candle coronets and singing soft prayers in Spanish by rote, by heart, by repetition — watched how those figures became flickering tokens as they joined the long line that glowed its way up the whitened grit and stony track, up to the sparse and grassy cementerio with its squat and small-belled adobe church and weathered, silver-gray grave-markers and ebonized crosses, chalky in the slumbering dust, as night-owls screeched in stands of lightly-stirring cottonwoods, ancient junipers and sticky piñon that overlooked the pious oncomers. They were a soft-streaming flow of attuned and fiery tenderness, there to feast with the spirits of their dead.

I turned back to the salon courtyard. It stood deserted. An evening wind lifted the tattered awnings. Abandoned ofrendas still glittered softly in the recesses, banked with slender wax tapers and small painted portraits and flower-heads floated in blackened terra-cotta pots. The altars seemed to elevate, eerily magic in the growing darkness, pearly buds of fire stippling the dusk. Wax flowed from those altar candles in morphing, fatted angels and night grotesques fed on oranges, corn and bread, quail eggs, horoscopy and spirit arroz.

And stray cats lingered, fighting. A man came out with a bucket of water and they scattered among the flickering altars. When he was gone they returned, cat-sore and volatile, picking their way through the half-empty stalls. . .

I sighed and turned. You could hear the spirit soldiers' roar from the crowded cantina and occasionally, a couple crossed the dirt plaza, hand-in-hand, looking for a place to go, but now the square was quiet again until I became aware of a soft clicking. In a corner of the courtyard sat an old lace-maker. Moving toward her, I saw the bobbins were fused finger-bones threaded with wire and Egyptian cotton. She deftly worked the web that was pillowed on her lap and images manifested, gleaming and white. In this danse macabre of delicate forms, an interlacing of small figures appeared: a girl with a dagger, a wagon on fire, a skeletal man on a pyre of bones — yarns intermingling in handcrafted symbols. I paused to watch her at her work, but she carried on as if unaware, her grimy fingers with their blackened nails rapidly developing each grim vignette. At length, I asked her what she was making.

'Mira,' she said, gesturing across the plaza to an old man crouched over his black lace piece, worked from cleverly spun aloe leaves. 'Mira,' she repeated, pointing to the corner opposite, where an elderly woman handled gold point d'Espagne, stuff of the old Inquisition banners, worked by the dim light of an ofrenda. Their threads were linked in a cobweb of pictures that slowly expanded across the worn flagstones and as I peered, there emerged more and more of these hunched figures, working their pillows over and over with cotton-threaded, clacking bones.

Then it seemed to me as if the threads were conjoined: ravelled or enmeshed with the garments of the ghosts — or perhaps were interwoven as the actual flesh and skin of these lace-making phantoms: mantillas of musculature and dirty hair, sabenquas of brain tissue, and lacily-issuing blood miasmas, and filagree tendons and venous tongues, and the colored silks of listening awareness and dyed sentience, and hand-worked memory itself, in an ever-expanding gossamer web that seemed a cocooning manifestation of the immaterial, the wild anatomy, the feral substance of ghost.

And then I saw that the lace-makers too, were depicted in this intricate dance of death, that they were intertwined as pictures of lace and with a sudden fear, knew not to seek out myself, my own portrait absurdly made in thread — but the old woman raised her work and I saw a man with a camera holding a scythe.

'No,' she said soothingly, lifting it off the pins, 'no para tí.' She patted my hand affectionately. Then the lace photographer became a palmful of threads, snipped at the base of their handworked life. She brushed the small tangle to the ground, but I picked it up and put it in my pocket and tipped her outstretched, expectant hand as if without those precautions, I'd no longer exist.

Then the moon rose: low, huge, gold and I started as the boy's hand brushed my own in a glow of unheated marrow, in the still-inviting touch of nocked carpal bones.

'It's time,' he said, and the scene changed as the courtyard filled with New Mexican stars hung high and hung low, as the milk trail burned in a frail constellation, as breath rose beneath it, fierce and fragile as smoke.

XVI

SÉANCE: E.E. HENRY PHOTOGRAPHIC STUDIO, LEAVENWORTH

Familiar spirit: Abner Jameson

WHERE DID PITY RESIDE on a night such as this, encircled by death? With the pious gone up to the grave-fields, the courtyard itself now sprang into life as if understudying Loma Parda's fate. Drunk spirits swung out through the salon's double doors. Crickets stung the stars. And the cribs dripped with sweat, as if dross skimmed from the villagers' now purified, religious emotion. All the while, the salon clamor kept up its musical vigil in a vigorously warped underscore. It was a song-fed garrison: oiled on lust, sated on smoke, sobered on dance.

A figure signalled to me: it was Jameson, pushed to the back of the crowd. He leaned against a wall, rolling a cigarette. 'Parmetar's gone and got himself killed,' he said, 'and this one's running on some strange fuel. I don't trust Browne as far as I could throw a chipped stone.' He spoke in a low murmur with the brim of his hat pulled right down: 'Look,' he said.

As if an invisible curtain had been stiffly raised, Browne now grubbed out the heavy, yellow trundle cart in front of the empty stalls and laid down his assorted props in a rough sphere on the uneven flagstones, setting up his stage within an imaginary circle whose circumference of quasi-magical straw and alchemical manure had been banked up by stable-boy apprentices, directed in stagecraft that seemed diabolical, until Browne came to reveal the half-rotted corpse he so fondly now thought of as his only son.

'He and Cosmo, both,' said Jameson.

A quadrant of torches flared in the wind and sparks showered on the spectral throng, vanishing into clothes of cotton, silk and linen — all fabrications, all miasmas of dust. And the bright, fierce paper costumes on a rough percussion of skeleton dancers now rustled and shimmied slightly, wired into darkness, as a light wind unsettled that dust.

Browne unclipped the makeshift front panel of his medicine cart and hooked it up, displaying half-filled bottles, bundles of feathers and dried flowers, fabric bolts, fireworks of all shapes and sizes, tool-boxes, a mattress, a stool and a piss pot.

'Looks like most of it hit that riverbed,' said Jameson.

Then the embalmer went to the stable to fetch the panther, and walked it round to the front of the crowd on a bit of rope. She padded softly, indolent now, and Browne had to yank her chain to make her snarl.

'Now watch this,' Jameson spat on the ground. 'Did you know about this?'

Browne stood, as if assessing the atmosphere, then slowly reeled the panther in. He stared at the crowd, threw back his head and let out a scream.

'She'd better respond,' said Jameson.

Browne screamed again and this time the panther joined him and the crowd stood silent before a scattered applause broke the tension.

'He'll pull a few stunts now, some fire-crackers and a cure-all,' observed Jameson.

Browne worked his makeshift stage and had the money cap ready to hand, posturing with his limited range of cures and preventions: 'But I think the best cure is invention, ladies and gentlemen: INVENTION. The good lord invented and now I present something to you further: REINVENTION. You might call it a sense of change or a death defiance or a point of argument but when you see his renewed face, his limbs as if full of life, you will be pointed in the correct direction as I give you now ROBERT MCGEE.'

'Hard to watch,' said Jameson. 'I'm going for a drink — want one?'

I shook my head.

There was a faint ripple of applause as Browne raised Allen Edwards' corpse. His face was waxen, blurred and honey-colored with faint shadowing. His eyelashes and hairline were like frayed silk: lustrous and softly textured, and the small bouquet wired lightly onto both wrists added a sensitive, formal touch. Browne replaced him in his open coffin and allowed the onlookers, one by one, to file past for the price of a coin.

'And so,' said Browne as the last of the curious trickled through, 'see him now brought to life again.' The embalmer replaced the coffin lid and then removed it to show the empty casket. The crowd seemed largely underwhelmed. Then he took the lid away again and there was a gasp among the gathering as the small body now stirred and slowly clambered out, speaking lines intoned from a small paper, his voice high and clear in the night air. Browne lifted Robert, boosting him high on his shoulder and carried him about, so that the boy could offer a view of his skull whilst Browne shouted out a wooden spiel of sorry tales and survivals, all the while holding out a soft hat that received chinking coins in its begrimed folds and when those metallic chinks thinned and the encircling torches steadied again, their hot air blurring, he set the living boy down to wild applause, whistles and clapping and roars, as the admiration of the throng crescendoed before an encore was called. Browne, striding round to the rear of the cart to collect up again his dead boy prop and put down his live boy prompt, took off his coat, went into the stable and stashed it in beneath the wagon seat along with the takings, and had a long drink of water and poured some over Edwards' corpse, and gave a little to Robert before beginning the act all over again.

Jameson waited in the stable shadows, careful of his own timing, before he lifted the rifle stashed alongside Bobby's makeshift bed, found ammunition tucked beneath the wagon-box, felt beneath the box-seat for Browne's folded overcoat and putting it on, pocketed several rolls of lint, and even more vials of morphine. Then he found the takings in an inner pocket of the coat and added to them the tips from the hat he'd taken from Bobby a little earlier. Weighed down on his right side by metal coins, he stood for a moment surveying the wagon-bed shelter that had been the boys' home for the past few weeks. Then he stepped down and away from the awning, as Browne once more called out for the boy to help, positioned the lantern, released the panther from her cage and watched her disappear.

It was a tired embalmer and exhausted boy who went through the motions for a fourth time that night: the crowd rowdier as the show went on — with Browne once calling the grand revelation to a halt. So, by the end of performance no. 4, he was well and truly done and took his last bow and made his last flourish and sold a few last bottles of strange-colored liquid and went round to the back of the stabled wagon with Edwards' body in his arms, noting a few small tears and openings in the boy's skin that would need tending to before the next day's performance, and lifting him into the back of the wagon, upset a small kerosene lamp which flared into quickened fire, catching the cuff of Allen Edward's jacket, then his thin arm, and then his small body, pumped full of arsenic and chemical flammables, the body that Browne then grappled with, desperate to fight it, this tornado of flames that encircled them both, as then the wagon-mule bolted with the wagon itself, pulled fast through that drunk and uproarious crowd.

All this occurred in smooth momentum, as if to meet the juncture of that fiery river, that external molten circumstance in which a mass of glass had broken into flame, and the faces of the ghostly women had grown tawny with fear, and a central bonfire in an upward torrent of yellow blaze and spark-licked air had swiftly consumed the figure of Browne — at last consigned to his ashy reinvention — who still gripped the boy, now an embrittling skeleton, as death fulfilled that smoke-led charm which rose to the stars as an unfortunate omen: a Loma Parda sign.

XVII
SÉANCE: E.E. HENRY PHOTOGRAPHIC STUDIO, LEAVENWORTH
Familiar spirit: Nathaniel Flint

'SIN DRIES SOCKETED ORBS in the unfused head bones of an infant skull, reads those flinty starlights above the charred Loma plaza, extinguishes all torches. Sin disperses human breath. Sin weighed that large and sudden crowd, counter-weighed that makeshift play. Sin brought forward action: slipped a blade in a rib-bone, twisted it — sighed. Sin recalled that action: raised a lantern to its cheekbone. Like so,' said a voice, as a flame scratched to life.

And in the ringed span of its halo I saw a raised scaffold on an outcrop of stone and on it reclined a skeletal man. He lowered his oil lamp, shielding its glow: 'You think this a cave, don't you? Look again,' he said, 'and you will find it is a tomb. The de Lopez family has been installed here for many generations. The other two caverns form votive chapels; benedictions signed off beneath the petroglyphs. There lies Carlos de Lopez and his troubled brother, Cosmo; their sister Catalina Alvina Chaireses who goes by her matrilineal names, but absent is Angelina, their young niece. She is, as you know, together with the other putas, one of the Peligros, at rest in their own charnel house. The catacumbas continue for miles, deep into the rock face. This is merely the de Lopez antechamber with its ofrendas, altares. . . cempasúchiles.'

He raised the lamp again and I saw we were in a high-walled cave, a natural stone cruciform. Gradually, as my eyes adjusted, I took in the many-piled bones: the huge skull mounds, row upon row of tibiae and femurs, until I was distracted by far-off voices, rising uneasily from the canyon's blackness. A traveling procession slowly advanced, faintly outlined by flame and song. I watched this steady conflagration make for the narrow river crossing as lanterns bobbed in that distant dark like a loosened bunch of bloodshot stars. Then, I turned back to the man.

'Come on up here,' he said, 'and sit with me, now.'

And there was something of my childhood Neighbor in him, this frail, emphatic figure of skin and bone, so that I went toward him, clambering up the rock.

'They will sing like that til dawn,' he said, as I topped his perch. He patted down a place to sit on the matted blanket and it seemed to me he was eagle-like, poised on a rickety eyrie, with a face that was bald and full of insights and eyes milk-haunted by distance.

'Tonight is the Día de los Angelitos, Day of the Innocents. Tomorrow, the Día de Muerto. Oh yes, these are grave-haunted quarters. Spirits are mostly seen retrospectively, clothed in their flesh — the attire of ghost — but a true spirit form would be more like a nebula of natural oils spread in ink water: a membrane of bejeweled and starry dust that is still mucosal, has a certain moistness of flesh to it. Some say the effect of the wind on trees and grasses and flames, is not the wind at all but that their movements are because of spirits passing. I cannot comment. I only live here with some of their clothing and the flowers placed to dress up that clothing.'

He gestured to a large enclave, lighting up a small clay pipe. And I saw the remains of a girl, tied to a cross-frame at the wrists and ankles; her skeleton still wearing a torn dress, her dark hair loose and dry-hanging and her skull was painted in Angel's

Trumpets with AMADA inscribed above her empty eye-sockets.

'The figure you are surveying is my adopted daughter, Elizabeth Flint de Lopez, raped and murdered by soldiers in eighteen-sixty. They tell me she was three months pregnant. I brought her here as a mere child of thirteen and she made her way with the other girls. Elisabeta, they called her. She was Cosmo's child bride and scarred from childhood burns. Could read the cave walls here as if they were testament texts. Sharp fingers. They caught her and tied her to a frame, as she is now. I should know, it was three winters before I discovered her corpse in a remote canyon, picked to bits by buzzards, only her bones remained. Her skeleton was fused to that scaffolding, as if she clung on. And so, my Elisabeta back came with me all of a piece. Dragged her like a travois behind my horse, gentle as I could. Ate her sins myself. Now she protects me. For as long as she remains here, I am permitted to stay.'

He paused, tapping ash from the pipe bowl. 'My name is Nathaniel Flint and I have been a Sin Eater all my life and my father before me and his father before him, gone back now all the generations I can recall and beyond those some more written down and beyond those the ones that were only recalled before yon pen and paper times. My Welsh ancestors brought over this custom with them to Patagonian smallholdings. I came out to Loma Parda for escape, tried to ply a different trade, but the old gift remained. Others heard of my services and I adapted the ritual for those who needed it. Consumed all the sins for miles around. And I have all those histories of eaten sin in my veins. None will touch the sins of the dead but I did my job, pasted in ash, living in seclusion. Survived from the meager takings. Arthritic, I survived the crop ruin of thirty-two by funereal matter alone. Cheeses and ales, sometimes whiskey, sometimes bread, was left out for me on cadaverous breastbones.'

He paused again, breathing heavily, and relit the small clay pipe. 'When you read your books at night, rub their pages with your listening fingers, they give comfort, but don't keep you from sin. Sin will sit within you like the blackened and pooling dregs in a pail and none will suck those up, no man nor beast: then the spirit finds itself bedraggled in death and soaked and it cannot escape that dross-water, that suffocating mud. So they call for me then and I come and I find the bread in-soaked with slops and the ale made of a yeasty sin, but I absorb them both — I'll drink a good sin down, I'll chew sin to pap, I'll take a gnarled sin of bone and crack it in my teeth.

Tis a hand-me-down set: someone else's suit of sins I get to have. Their sins are not abstract to me: I feel every wrongdoing like a moral canker. I besmirch and besmirch: my house of pain is heavy with a dais of woodworm, heavy with a rotted truss: my head is not hung in shame, but in sin, and slowly the dark work of it all detuned my bones, unworked my muscles so that I became thus thin and thus rangy-hearted. I see it all in dream, the passing of their incontinent wills. My nerves take on their fears, their horrors, and I am weighed with consequence.

There's time in the space between expiration and the soul's departure. The passing time. Tis written into all clock mechanisms, whether water or metal, or with a wooden gong, or in the measured sweep of the sun's finger-shadow. Because caught between two points of a maze: that interval in which a death starts and ends — when the spirit still traces the mortal walls, blindfold, hunting for the leopard, hunting for the lamb, and death comes redoubled: the great sacrificial bull and great sacrificer: man — can I help their dualism? Help the bull become the man and the man become the bull again? Help the drab phoenix, make her literate with flame? Help the wary unicorn tip, guide its point to the poison cup, help the silvered haunch of beast, quivering toward its death? Somewhere on the outskirts of the labyrinth lies that blemished horn of time, abandoned on its leather shackle: toxins of banishment still drying out. . .'

Flint's most-meager and most-needed meal, he recalled, was consumed for the sins of a very young girl, shrunken-headed with pale silk tresses whose veins stood out like a tangled, blue copse from her folded, death-heavy arms. This was Elisabeta's younger sister, laid out in a Leavenworth parlor. Only four years old. He had performed the prayer:

'I give easement and
rest now to thee, dear
child. Come not down the
lanes or in our meadows.
And for thy peace, I
pawn my soul.
Amen.'

'On her chest,' said Flint, 'a thimble, for want of other metal, had been placed. Nearby, a half-shot of bourbon and a scant crock of gruel.'

Half-famished, he had devoured. Recalled Elisabeta's brother wouldn't release her, kept gripping Laura's hand as they lifted the bier.

'Well, Elisabeta clear ran off with me, then. Found her in the back of the wagon, some twenty miles on. Must have heard me tell her brother I was headed out here. That Parmetar household was surely a strange one.'

I started: 'Her brother, you say?'

'Aye.' He blinked.

'I prepared that young body to be photographed in Leavenworth. Yes, Laura Parmetar, I remember her now.'

'Perhaps you might tell me of it,' said Nathaniel, 'as you help light these tapers ahead of us.'

Seemed there were hundreds there, spread across the cave floor at the feet of this dried Madonna, this Elisabeta, spread out in a carpet of collapsing knots of stellar gas and dust. I bent down, dipped my flame like a kiss to each waiting wick. I told Flint of webs and how then, we were interlinked: James, Elisabeth and Laura Parmetar and myself to Laura, having taken her post-mortem likeness — 'here in this, studio' — and so had connections to Flint, who had adopted Elisabeth and to the estranged Cosmo, who married and impregnated her and then to Angelina, whose useless blood vengeance had snuffed Parmetar's understanding — 'but perhaps it was for the best,' interrupted Flint, sitting upright on his palette, 'perhaps it was only for the best' — as now we reflected on this dead girl, Elisabeta, for whom Parmetar drank and pined, for whom Cosmo lost his wits and — 'for whom I,' said the Sin Eater, 'grew very weary in spirit and soon began the will to die. This, an insolvency of experience,' he said, 'a deep-frustrated end. All those who would return to her, slowly turned away.'

The candles glowed in the dark.

'Could we summon her?' I asked at length.

'We could,' said Flint. 'We could attempt it.'

Outside, the singing throng had advanced. Raised high on the putas' shoulders, was the stabbed corpse of Captain Parmetar.

'They will bury him tonight,' said Flint, gazing into the distance. 'If we raise Elisabeta, then we should also raise Parmetar. Have them meet.'

'And you will eat his sin?'

'A last gesture. . . ' Nathaniel mused and he jerked sharp clangs from a bell with a rough hanging rope by his bed. 'The old adobe church bell was installed here a century ago and its tongue is still willing to lick out some peels.'

I covered my ears as he pulled and pulled, half-lifted out of his litter, sometimes hauled up a little, as if to swing out into the darkness beneath that metal bell whose hollow sounded harsh, violent and inevitable.

'Now they will come,' he panted, letting the braided rope slip from his hands, 'now they will come to us.'

Like a laval flow slowly re-routed, the singing crowd now advanced toward the cave mouth. When the procession entered, I saw the villagers in detail: the dark eyes, the head squares, the pockmarks, the sleeping children and atop all this, Parmetar's corpse that seemed to float like the corpse of a saint, paler than sunlight, and it sweated slightly with light beads that still clung to his lifeless face. Silence fell as the villagers watched the Sin Eater rise from his dirty pallet.

'Pan,' he said. The villagers passed a bundle along a line of careful hands and up into his own.

'Cerveza,' he said, and it was provided.

When he came down the rock he looked a ragged desert stylite toppled by a storm wind who stood for a moment with hands upraised over Parmetar's lifeless body. Then he knelt and prayed a small and startling prayer, his head pressed to the corpse's abdomen as if listening for an unborn child. He had tenderly broken the bit of bread and laid it on Parmetar's breastbone and the beer was placed at the corpse's side and Nathaniel Flint partook of both, ingesting them with white-rolled eyes, taking them methodically and wholly and without rushing. Then he staggered to his feet again and they helped him up to his scaffold.

'Déjame por un tiempo,' he said, 'leave him for the night — come and take him tomorrow.'

And so they departed, peaceful and silent, back down to the Loma gravesides for food and prayer and sunrise.

'I am tired now,' Flint said, 'too tired for spirit resurrections. But I can tell you about tonight's events, how she caught them out there on the mountain track, Jameson and the boy, pointed out the way up here and gave them dead cakes and a bottle of ale and they took them with gratitude, not knowing this was not a parting gift. "Cuevo tres," she'd insisted, holding up three boney digits. They, worn out and needing a place to sleep and think, trudged on up and found me in darkness. Catalina followed, having worked out the thing in that wily old brain of hers: "Estas cuevas siempre han albergado cosas, animales salvajes, hombres y mujeres salvajes," she'd said to me, peering right into my face. "Veo que tu tambien tienes desenfreno and," she had added in her careful English, "is always better to let wild things go."

"Old woman," I then had said to her, "I need this from you like air in a shadow." Yet for me there had only been one question. My mind, my shambolic mind, knew how to eat sin but for most else was deteriorated. My flesh was cankered and already falling from the sinews and at night the coyotes knew it and the midday shadows had become cast by buzzards as I hid in here, enveloped by bones. No-one forgives an old man. No-one ever asks the question: who will consume the Sin Eater's sins?

Well, I shall tell you now: Abner Jameson ate up my sin under threat of gunfire earlier tonight. Then I retrieved my old bone, carved with interval holes to blow the fundamental note of the flute. I knew how to sound that death note and perished on its piercing whistle. I can tell you that Jameson died in the Utah wilderness in 1887. Had lived, shacked up in a pen out there. Some say, on his arrival, a storm blew in — or rather, blew him into that community of sheep herders and lapsed Mormons — a bewildered weather that drove sanded stalks into chaff and a voluminous dust that covered person and beast and dwelling, so that all took on the appearance and properties of furious tatterdemalions. They say Jameson brought that bad storm in, as a spirit destitution. But scapegoat to scapegoat he wandered freely. I know of such small compensations.' He paused to cup the ash-gray pipe.

'And the embalmer?'

'Dead. Burnt up in the wagon trying to lift out the body of Edwards.

'And the boy?'

'If I were God,' he said, 'who I am not — not least because no god ever felt this weary — though I stand in parody of the first deity to become an altar sacrifice: if I were God, I should find their smoke and blood appalling. Those visceral worships. Goat to goat, I still paced on the ingested wilderness of sin, the landscape within that bewildered heart of damage, until giving it to him — the man, Jameson. Yes, we locked our spiritual horns.'

'And the boy?' I said again.

'Let me now still them,' said Flint, fidgeting in his bed clothes, 'this, after all, is a shadow-house of death and death still moves though most would have it hold quite still. Death stirs with its own life. Like an agitation in mud-grounded water. Stirs up those clouds.'

I shifted on my haunches.

'Yes, the boy,' said Nathaniel dazedly. 'Look at him there, how will he grow? He watched Jameson feed from my breastbone: the dead cakes, the ale, heard him say the necessary prayers and get up very slowly, as if from a low table, a wild look in his eye then: something made of assuaged violence and so the boy drew back, afraid. Ah yes, I saw it. Like the growing momentum of a torpid, underwater wind. This, after I sounded the note of the flute. Then I removed my garments of skin and bone — inhabit them now only when being watched or summoned — and drove my freshened spirit up to the aerated waters, the mountain springs of wonder and solitude. I was a ghost-clot by then. Only then, did Catalina take the boy — she who would die in her lonely sleep, dreamless, friendless — take the boy by his thin and trembling hand and walk cave-ward into deep recesses of fire-lit bone, down those cramped osseous corridors, as I watched the flame recede between them.'

XVIII

SÉANCE: E.E. HENRY PHOTOGRAPHIC STUDIO, LEAVENWORTH

Familiar spirit: Jack Denton

'I DID NOT POSSESS the wolf in my heart on that particular railroad journey to Flagstaff — even within the blizzard, during which I'd survived those three long weeks on raw chicken eggs and snow. Nor did I keep the wolf heart-clenched afterward, though I'd witnessed an ice-wet and dog-wild scene through a lens breathed into clarity on the railway car windowpane. That wolf, I called the Summoning Wolf and it was the beast which occupied my dreams the most — though the wolf I was then to kill, oftentimes joined him. She was lithe and hawkish and dun-colored — and she moved like smoke. El Fantasma: a creature who lived out her life on those high-rolling plains of my rusted dreams.'

A spirit moved forward into the room.

'Jack Denton,' he said. 'I was on a winter job, like many others I'd wintered on. It was a big hustle, but paid well. Wolves had been my livelihood oh, for about forty years or so by then and I took it upon myself to say I knew their habits well. But maybe the Summoning Wolf was a foreshadowing, a kind of premonition. Maybe he showed me how El Fantasma would work out. Sure, you can always kill them but somehow still, you've always lost. They'll look right through you. Because you're a coward and a cheat — especially if you're only after the pelt. Probably protecting corralled livestock, those heifers and calves, is mostly different. But to go out there and bring a wolf down for fur or sport. . . well, it'll shrivel up a good part of yourself — it'll shrivel up your heart. So when I say I didn't have the wolf in my heart, it was because I was pretty well heart-wizened by then. Not much room left to take anything in. But though not heart-possessing, these two wolves did possess my dreams: dreams of the utmost peril, I still remember having.

Denton pulled off his heavy gloves and sat down at the studio table.

'Now go sleeping in those snow-drenched woods with me,' he said, leaning right in. 'Watch that powdered white woodpile. The stalled train. The whole night, stilled. When the blizzard calms, the view from this frozen, wooden car will be glittering: a dense diamond ground beneath a liquid moon. Your breath-mark on the windowpane will seem to expand and contract like a lunar mirage. Everything will hold an intense quality of listening. The wolf's about to enter my wolf-skinner dream. . .'

'Well, I'll be damned,' said a voice nearby, as someone coughed. 'Would you look at that.'

Some strange spurt work was happening in the snowy bitterness. Short shadows shifted fast among the trees and something crawled, or seemed to crawl, across our line of vision in a heavy mark.

'Take a seat,' said Denton to this new observer.

'Thanks,' said the other.

All else were asleep.

'What do you see?'

'Nothing. Nope, nothing likewise.'

A febrile and squeaky rubbing with a glove restored a better sightline to the glass.

'Moon's so damn bright.'

'Snow's brighter.'

'Look,' said the man. 'Look,' he whispered gently, 'here they come. That's a big pack of wolves.'

'They're dogs, not wolves,' murmured Denton.

'How d'you know?'

I heard the disappointment in the passenger's voice.

'Oh, shape, size, kind of movement, kind of feel. Now *that*,' Denton pointed, 'is a wolf.'

The large animal had dragged itself up onto the soaking, black mound, slipping and snarling. There was a pause and then the dog pack congealed in one aggressor movement.

'Gonna see them off?'

'Don't know,' said Denton. 'Doubt it. Never seen a wolf before?'

'Not like this, I haven't. Look how they're surrounding him,' said the passenger.

'Yep, and they'll get him, too. Must be some sort of local pack got loose. Those are large hounds,' said Denton, as the dogs closed in on the wolf and even from that distance, barking and growling could be heard in the white clarity of the winter acoustics.

'Did it last an hour, I later considered,' said Denton, turning to me again, 'or was it only moments in which the wolf stood, flaring with violence and saw the dogs off one by one: stood high on a shifting log pile in the glittering, moonlit dark? And what was it to my heart when there was a pistol crack from the caboose and the wolf lay dead? The dog pack got broken up. Another and another went down. Three dogs had fallen and a passenger trudged out to claim them, skinning their carcasses in the moon-living night. With the spark from a flint I ignited a bundle of old newspapers and lit a railcar bench someone had already worked over, chopping it into chips. More passengers came out to the fire to get some warmth and then to eat. We divided up that meat, fresh-hot, among us. And that night,' said Denton, 'when the train suddenly got moving, it was as if our Roman-seeming ritual had loosened up the gauged metal from its snow-locked sockets — and we were free, but changed.' He lit up a cigarette.

'Now, I always take that winter dream along with me, night and day. And if I do dream it in my sleep, then I wake with the smell of that fire and the wolf flesh, roasting. You see, for me, though that wolf staved off my starvation. . . it was just a prolonged passing. Because it marked a beginning: wolf to wolf. My real death had started somewhere near Flagstaff and fetched up in the de Chelly canyon.'

XIX

SÉANCE: E.E. HENRY PHOTOGRAPHIC STUDIO, LEAVENWORTH

Familiar spirit: Jack Denton

'FLAGSTAFF DEPOT WAS DIRT-COLD and dormant. Few trains passed through and when I stepped down,' Denton said, 'I took nothing particular in but the high blue cold air as I slowly crossed those empty double tracks with the other dazed and travel-sore companions. I'd several boxes of ammunition, two Marlin .44 rifles, my Winchester and cartridges, a small satchel of watercolors and paper, a camera, apothecary vials of arsenic and strychnine, pre-prepared gelatine capsules, cowhide gloves and knives, hypodermic needles, notebooks, rope lengths, four lassoes, a wolf hunting guide, and ten Newhouse Special 4 1/2 wolf traps plus chains, but my battered journal I kept on me, kept it close. Most else kitted out a pair of heavy trunks and leaving these with the porter, I made my way over to the newly-built DeMonte hotel to wait there, as the letter instructed, ordered bread and fresh coffee and killed another quarter hour before the rancher got in, stamping snow off his boots, clapping together his gloved hands. He brought a whole host of snow in with him and the bare boards were wetted with his footprints, just as those same boards had begun to dry out again from my own. See — here he comes, now.'

The new spirit looked around, searchingly. I watched as his expression changed and he trudged over to Denton, pulled back a chair, and sat down. He had a pockmarked face and large, discerning, black eyes that had seen too much and now selected what it was he saw exactly in his recollecting mind's eye.

'Frank Borla,' he said. 'Got your wire yesterday. Coffee —'
he motioned and the bartender acknowledged him. 'So,' he said,
'— Denton?'

'Call me Jack,' said Denton, lighting a cigarette.

'Good, thank you,' Borla said to the spirit coffee-giver and
blew on the steaming cup. 'Jack,' he said, getting down to it. 'We
have us an unusual problem. How much did Abarca fill you in?'

'Enough for me to come on down.' Denton pulled a letter
from his inner coat lining and laid it on the table in front of
Borla.

'Yes,' Borla spoke as he read, 'yep, that about does it. When
was this sent?' He turned the letter over and back again.

'Some two months ago.'

'Okay, well, you can gauge for yourself the weather's set in —'
he took a gulp of coffee, '— forgive me, your journey was — ?'

'Badly delayed. Got trapped in that snow for near-on three
weeks.'

Borla eyed Denton: 'Thought your telegram came mighty
late. Was beginning to think you weren't coming at all. You gonna
be all right for this?'

'A good kip and a hot bath'll sort me out.'

'We'll rest up here tonight, anyways. Then tomorrow set on
out early. It'll be rough going but shouldn't be more than a couple
of days. Brought a horse for you and got the cart out back —
that's yours, I take it?' He pointed at Denton's kit bag.

'Yep. Left both trunks at the depot.'

'And we'll have more supplies at the ranch for you. Want to
eat?'

'Like to wash up first.'

'Fine, good. Shall we say six o'clock then.'

'Done. And my trunks?'

'I'll have them brought over from the station now.' Borla rose abruptly and downing his coffee, left.

Denton watched him go through the bar-front window, heard the whistle as a wolfhound followed him. Looking both ways, Borla crossed Chestnut Street as if it were a snow-filled gulley and the hound flanked him, limping in the slush.

I thought again on the wolf: its black mouth open in the dark, the dogs twisting down on its violent body. Wondered what kind of sign this was to Denton now, as the light was lowering and he drowsed a little over the bread and coffee remains, then came to as Borla recrossed the road.

'They're bringing them over, he said, stamping into the hotel bar, filling the room with snow-cold air. 'Now for our rooms — no, no — you stay there.'

'Thanks,' Denton yawned, 'I'm fair beat.'

'I can see it,' the rancher said.

And I discerned the particular warmth in his voice amongst other voices emanating from the dimly-lit hotel foyer as reservations were made and Borla re-emerged — 'They say we should eat first,' he said and shrugged.

The dining room was near-empty when they began and deserted when they finished. Dinner was served across four courses and then they drank a good claret.

'This might be the last outpost of luxury we'll ever meet,' said Borla, clipping a cigar. He offered the hunter one.

'I have my own.' Denton said and took one carefully from its foil package and tapped it vigorously on the table top. Then he rubbed his forehead, lit the thing and sat back to smoke it.

'Yes, it isn't without some risk,' said Borla, presently. 'We had the loup-garoup fella down with his salt charms and garlic, by the name of Laroche. . . and then of course, there was Flannery.'

'Flannery?'

'Brought in wolfhounds — that bitch you saw with me today was left with us to heal, too damaged to travel on. Of the six, two survived,' said Borla, 'but I understand you take a different approach. I read your pamphlet.'

'Yes,' said Denton, 'it's all in the scent.'

Borla poured them another glass of wine. 'How so?' he said, politely.

'Well, you must know about smell, how it lingers, when it travels, where it wanders. We leave our own stench everywhere. Our scent marks here, for example, are on every spoon, glass, cup, side plate, on every chair we sit upon; on bar tops, table tops and — most importantly for me — on our clothing.'

'You have a system.'

'I have a system,' Denton said, 'and it is this: blood and binding. Anything I touch, whether preparing kidneys or strychnine or cheese — anything — from traps to rope, I touch with gloves soaked in heifer's blood. I have a special blood suit that I put on before even beginning and I keep it hung up in an outhouse, separate from human things. Then, I use blood-soaked gloves that have been allowed to dry out and I keep a scarf over my mouth so that none of my breath reaches the kit or bait. I ride out in this suit and am careful not to dismount, and when I have to, I have blood-soaked boots, but I keep my blood-soaked gloves on all the time, never take them off. And that's how I do it. Simply put, I become the smell of blood.'

'The ranchers won't like it,' Borla said.

'No?'

'No. But I'm all prepared to defend your methods, Denton. Truth is, they've begun to fully believe what they'd half-convinced themselves of anyway, which is that we're dealing with something infernal, an animal of greater cunning than any have previous dealt with out here. Take the band, for example. All are larger lobos than average, all evade the bullet, all kill for pleasure. There's a yellow wolf and there's a black wolf, both young. Then there's the smoke-colored one. The Mexicans have taken to calling that wolf, El Fantasma.'

'You've seen him?'

'Seen *her*,' said Borla, 'she camped out in a cave at the cliff base opposite my cabin for near on six months. Right under my nose. I confess for a while there, I was as uneasy as the ranch hands. Started to take the shape of her name.'

'No such thing.'

'No such thing, but maybe she became what they believed she was.'

There was a small chink of china as another diner discretely departed. Smoke rose between the two men.

'I think no such thing is possible, Mr Borla. Intelligence, yes. Memory, yes. Hunger, yes. Devilry? In a wolf? No. Not in all the demon races run, have I met such a runaround as a bright wolf will give you. Yet, I remain convinced that they are creatures just the same as any other in the animal realm and as such, I shall continue to kill them.'

'You speak like a poet, sir.'

'Merely a painter.'

Borla tilted his head.

'I observe and draw and oftentimes, paint.'

'And hunt.'

'And hunt when there is need, or sometimes simply to document. Birds are fleeting.'

Borla finished his wine. 'As are wolves,' he said and moved to get up. 'I'll call for you at six tomorrow morning.'

'I'll be ready,' Denton said.

#

SÉANCE: E.E. HENRY PHOTOGRAPHIC STUDIO, LEAVENWORTH

Familiar spirit: Frank Borla

BEFORE DAWN, I RODE out with the men. We took the rough track made by the ganaderos who'd carved out the route with repeated crossings. Sometimes sleet, sometimes rain, insoaked the air. Clouds already full with snow had gathered on some distant bluffs, and the flap and call of crows hung in the darkness. Across two days we rode out that track, bedding down by a cookfire in the wintry scrubland. On the clear afternoon of the third day, the trail veered off and a dilapidated cabin stood just ahead of us.

'This is it,' Borla said, his breath pale in the freezing air. 'Will do?'

'Do me just fine,' Denton dismounted, 'if there's an outbuilding.'

'Got a barn and outhouse both. You go on in. I'll take care of the horses.' He unhitched the two horses from the wagon and untethered Denton's and led them to the barn and patted them down and gave them their feed bags and threw a blanket over each one and watched them for a moment. Pale gold afternoon sunlight cut a slant across his face and I felt its warmth. Then he stepped back out into the cold again and pulled the barn door to, securing it hard.

'Denton —' he called, moving across the sunlit ground. The cabin door stood ajar. 'Denton?' He crossed the threshold and pushed the door open.

'Steady,' came Denton's voice, 'steady now,' he warned, but Borla had already drawn his gun.

The wolf-hunter cupped his hands and Borla stepped forward, lowering his weapon. He looked in Denton's careful palms and saw a beady-eyed plover furred with dull feathers.

'What will you do with it?' He holstered the gun. 'Paint it?'

'I will set it on its way,' replied Denton, slowly advancing toward the cabin door.

But it wouldn't go, and the cold air further chilled an already frozen hut. Denton drew the bird back in and set it down on the table top. He stood, contemplating it, then said, 'I shall call you Merchiston.'

'What in god's hell kind of a name is that,' Borla muttered, wandering about, turning things. 'Them boys of Jose Abarca's didn't leave this place too good. I'll have to speak with him. Okay,' he said abruptly, turning to Denton, 'let's unload while the light's still good. Brought some dried cottonwood bark for the horse. I got cordwood and logs for you, and some dried out sage brush for kindling, should keep you at least a month, but I'll be back before then anyways.' Borla talked as they moved out to the cart, and then flung back the awning. 'Got you some tins of fruit and preserved apples, flour, coffee, bacon, biscuits, molasses, tobacco, paraffin oil, wool blankets and ink.'

'Like I asked for.'

'Like you asked for. Also, paper. There's the bait for the traps in wax paper and I'm having a young heifer delivered over to you in the next day or so. You can keep her cooped up in the barn.'

'Many thanks,' Denton said. He paused. 'Might you have got me any soap?'

'Yup. Plenty of it.'

'Good,' Denton said, and started hauling.

Come two o'clock the hut was stacked up.

'Shall leave you to it,' Borla said. 'I'm keen to make tracks. I'll reach Jose's by nightfall if I set off now. Here's a hand-drawn map of the area, the creek's due north — Marshall Creek — and here's the Mitchell map. I've plotted it out for you. She does a wide loop around the Nova Grande circuit, but you'll soon get to know her ways. How long did you and Abarca agree on?'

'Could be weeks, could be days,' Denton said, 'but I've committed to a good two months.'

Borla nodded. 'Sure is striking country out here. I know all say it. It ain't a wilderness, it's a place of sunlit ghosts. I near quit some mornings out near the Marshall. Used to feel all here were varmints, save the cattle. Cattle like some kind of holiness itself, to be preserved. 'Course the holiness is in the cash. Truth is, those wolves ain't got nothing much else to live on, or live for, all told. No buffalo. All hunted off. That cattle's just standing around waiting to be devoured. Like the anger of the buffalo entered the wolf and the wolf is out to tell us so. Most would say this is damn foolish nonsense. Well, I'll be on my way.' He paused, rangy with feeling. 'All I can say is, I wish to the core of my old battered bit of heart you don't catch her. That wolf's earned her keep, is all.'

'I hear you,' Denton said.

Borla squared him for a moment. 'Adios,' he tipped his hat. 'There'll be a hand come down in a couple of days with that heifer. Just let him know if there's anything else you're after and we'll oblige.' And so saying, he did up his collar and drew his hat down and went across to the barn and led out the mares and hitched them up as the first snowflakes of the afternoon started slowly circling.

And all the time Denton stood on the makeshift stoop, watching him. The day was beginning to turn then, as mist rose on the hills like smoke and thin-toned calls of wolves rose also on that frozen air as the men paused for a long moment, listening to them.

'Go easy, Denton,' Borla mounted his horse. 'Go easy, now. Don't let that phantom wear you out.'

Denton nodded. 'Thank you for all,' he said and then turned and pushed the cabin door closed.

'And that was the last I did see of him before he died in that canyon fall,' said Borla to me, leaning forward in the saddle to soothe his horse, 'and before I was then become dead also. Adios,' he said. 'If you can, keep an eye on him.'

And the rancher rode out softly then, softly into the enfolding snow.

XXI

SÉANCE: E.E. HENRY PHOTOGRAPHIC STUDIO,
LEAVENWORTH

Familiar spirit: Jack Denton

DENTON STOOD QUIET IN the cabin as a shrill wind
penetrated its badly-stuffed timbers and in the half-light watched
his breath bloom like a spectral mold, before vanishing. I felt he
knew this quietude, this smell of emptiness and so stood for a long
while — as if that hush was tantamount to a slow transfusion of
old and familiar silences from childhood — before eventually he
moved. Glass littered the floor where a pane had gotten smashed
so that he crossed the boards in a crunching gait to crouch down
by the sheet-iron stove in an attempt to get it lit. Nothing doing.
Old embers like the remains of a sunken ship sat in their cold
and greasy ash, refusing the match and so, cussedly, he took a
shard of glass and scraped out the stove, chucking the cremated
stumps onto the snow where they lay like charred and useless
glyphs, as he made his way to the outside barn and returned with
a cordwood bundle and sage-wood faggot and bust them open
and laid a new fire with a flint-struck flame and rootling in his kit
box got out the dented coffee pot and wiped it out and measured
a coarse grain into its base and set it down on the stove for a
moment to retrieve a tin cup — equally battered, equally vital —
which he then filled from the cabin stoop with handfuls of drift
beneath the lancing snow: once, twice, eight times over, before
carrying that holy snow-cup back across the glittering floor.

The plover watched him.

Denton softly cursed again: 'Realizing,' he grumbled at me,

'I didn't ask the whereabouts of the well.' And so trudged out to locate it and came in again, banging the door hard both ways and rummaged around in behind some old sackcloth and got himself a metal pail and trudged out again as all the while distant wolves howled. It was a thin type of dusk and the sound of the well crank was rusted and loud in the air. Denton banged back in with the brimming pail and filled a pan with water and boiled himself up a few potatoes. He sat down in the rocker by the window and pushed his boots off across the best part of ten minutes. Then he poured himself a cup of coffee and another, before shoving on those loosened boots again to bang back out into the snow and took a long leak from the snow-filled cabin stoop (it having been some several hours now, as he focused on the dull treeline, enduring its wet plumps of snowfall) and having done so, now up-buttoning a cold-stiffened trouser seam, looked up to find a wolf standing some eleven feet or so off, in the blurring and fast-obliterating snow.

Denton backed off real slow, real careful. He padded back, slow to the door, slow-reversing into the cabin and reached for his rifle and loaded it and went to the broken paned window-frame whose jagged glass gave a crude rest for the muzzle. He found the wolf still standing, motionless: concurrent. It watched him for a long moment, before moving off. Denton fired as if in salute, then let the gun rest and waited, but the wolf was alone.

Behind him the stove fire had dwindled and Denton increased the draw and stoked it and boiled up the coffee again for the last of its dark suds and then he set about putting the place to rights. In the bucking glow of four oil lamps I watched him move about the hut as the last of the daylight slipped fully now into the wicklight's realm. He fixed a faded watercolor of wolves to the worn timber wall, switching it for a framed Lord's prayer and he brushed the uneven floor planks clear of chunks of glass and dead leaves, varmint scat and cobwebs, leaving them in a crude and unlikely bonfire on the inner side of the outer door: 'For the morning,' he said, 'never so good to cross a wolf in the dark. . .'

He slotted his books onto a small and rickety shelf with his paintbox and pads: the guns were stashed on their bone hooks above the door and one half of the sturdy and calloused square pine centre-table he designated to kitchen supplies, only to find inset shelves veiled by burlap behind an open inner door and so then stepped into the other, smaller room — darker than the first, with its crude cot and damp-seeming mattress, cracked washstand and clouded mirror hung beneath a warped and small, whittled crucifix: evidence of the Catholic shepherds, I thought — stepped into this defeated antechamber whose contents smelled of a woodpile musk, of hunter sweat and herder persistence, of the wild log of cobwebbed winters: stepped forward, the crook of his left arm stuffed with two woolen blankets, his right hand wielding a flickering lamp and took in the room's cramped dimensions, noted the balding calfskin floor coverings, the small bedside table (useful for coffee, un-useful for a bible) and saw above the bedstead also, someone had fixed a sconce for reading by and so seeming to have assessed the place, Denton now crossed the room, tipping the blankets onto the bed and went to shutter its snow-slatted windows.

It was only then that he noticed, crouching to bring the lamp to the splines, how worn the lower wall planks beneath the window had become, how marked the boards were there with repeated crossings and now, standing to close the rough-hewn shutters and grasping the oil lamp, whose glow was partly reflected in the window pane, he saw for a long and cold moment a face in the beyond that was not his own, that was not a true reflection or snowy, kerosene mirage, that was not his fatigue or the return of the rancher, Frank, (that was not even the faint outline of my own watchful face), but that his flickering lamp had illuminated it first — before he even locked eyes with it, the pale being framed on the outer side of the window glass that stared back at him for that prolonged moment and vanished.

He snuffed the flame quick-smart.

Twice, an element in the darkness. Twice, a failure for recompense. Then he lowered the lamp globe and glass tapped glass in an unknown code as the snow swirled on.

'Nothing there to see,' Denton said to himself, 'nothing there to see out there in that darkness.' He pulled the shutters to and bolted them with a blunt sound and took the oil lamp back to the solid table, reloaded his weapon and re-entered the night.

Then the spirit shepherds came to rest, watching us, as Denton returned from circling the barn and having found nothing, tiredly put another pot of coffee on. The night was warmed with its fragrant darkness and in that darkness he polished his gun.

XXII

SÉANCE: E.E. HENRY PHOTOGRAPHIC STUDIO,
LEAVENWORTH

Familiar spirit: Jack Denton

NEXT MORNING, HE ROSE at five and the snow-flecked air was muted and calm as Denton breakfasted and gave the horse her feed in the high, clear light of the barn. He got kitted out and saddled up and by six was out on the trail with the map and broke that trail at a gulley by a copper stand of cottonwoods as the sun rose in a furious gold: older and wise. And in its heat the snow now crept back, revealing black and dormant moss banks. The day was grown from pooled darkness like pale fire in the long trek around. Early sunlight lay flattened in the grasses beneath the drifts.

He walked that trail of booming pine soil with its small flocks of chaffinches and passed through pale cerulean shadows and from the snow-drifted plain, surmounted the barren high points, noting down the landmarks the ganaderos used. The air held clear as he surveyed the valley for nearly fifty miles about in a vast flank of snow-swept ground. From this position, you could clearly see a sliver of the canyon, deep and chalky-red and cloaked in creamy patches of snow. Denton gradually tracked down into that canyon whose walls rose reddish and blunt in the midday light. A river glinted through, between clusters of fruit trees that stood stark in the winter air. The place had a tranquil atmosphere as if peace itself were watching over him there.

'I'll make out these routes when we get in,' Denton said to me, as the light was now fading and he beat back along the trail.

'Then I'll have a good nose for the ground on paper. The snow's an ally, will help to read the wolf's intent.'

Denton stayed put that afternoon, finished working over Borla's maps and charts with colored waxes to plot out ten sites for the wolf traps. The plover sat in a paper bullet box and he fed it softened bits of bread, working over its lines in chalk and in-filling those lines with watercolor. Sometimes he sat, brush in one hand, cigarette in the other, pausing to survey first the paper plover, then the flesh plover. Sometimes he slowly turned through the end pages of his battered journal looking for points of comparison, reminders, sample palettes. He was wise-seeming and doleful and the waxy oil-light heightened the concentration in his grizzled features, I thought. Now and again, he'd cast an eye over the outdoor scene as the light sank to dimness, but he kept those hut shutters open like sight-lines in a fort as he wrote up his day in the flickering light:

<u>Monday January 18th, 1890</u> — You could not ask for a better fellow than Frank Borla and it is a deep regret that we will not be working out here together as I find I have a real rapport with this kindred rancher-hunter. It's a fair set up out here and I have enough provisions to get me through the worst of it, thanks to Borla. Been clear someone's about, however. Whether a shepherd checking things over or a vagrant looking for a kip-pad, I'll keep an eye out. Good to extend the hand of friendship, in any case until I get it ironed out. I think the wolf maybe also came to check me out. It was too dark to see the true color of its hide and snow bewilders scale so that I couldn't make out whether it was a male animal or even the phantom herself, deviant and trouble-wild. Will get a proper look soon, no doubt. I notice the need to build up some muscle in my legs again — am aching after the ride out. But I am ready for this next

part of things. The world out here is an untamed wilderness indeed, and rich in its wildlife. Today I took the trail for the first time. Clouds of snow on the horizon, none of which cared to fall and a jackrabbit or two. Crows in the trees. Sun-fall on the crisp ground. Serene. It's a good long trail, some six miles or so and it runs along the edge of the canyon and then down into its steep-walled valley. I came across a man on a horse in the shrubs but though he paused for a moment to observe me, he merely raised a hand before trotting off. I would have liked to speak with him. I watched his long dark hair flick in the cold wind. Then I turned up-canyon and tracked the river edge for a while, before taking the track back up again to finish the loop. Somewhere, she has a den in the bluffs or in the cliff caves or perhaps even along the riverbank. I saw a few signs of movement, some scat, but nothing much else. Most of the trail lies above the canyon, only dipping down into it for half a mile or so. I write this as owl brethren hoot outside, with cramped fingers and a real need for sleep.

Some time toward five — I guessed — a thin nickering came through the darkness and Denton got up, immediately alert. He snuffed the oil lamps in the room, took up his gun and went to the window opposite the barn to settle down there waiting, as I crouched alongside him. Earlier in the afternoon, he'd gone ahead and lit the barn lantern and it now gave the outdoor scene an uneasy, theatrical feeling.

'There was a prairie fort captain,' he said to me in a low voice after a while, 'can't recall his name, but he was something of a one. Drunkard. His men went out shooting for sport. One day, brought back a wolf cub with them and this captain took it on, nurtured it — gave it milk and jackrabbits and jerky, that kind of thing. Got to be grown a full three years and would howl at night. The company couldn't cope with it howling and howling and, though I heard that captain was near reduced to tears, the wolf was turned loose. Next day he rode out, caught up with it in a plum tree bluff and shot it through the head. Knew it didn't have a chance out there and wanted its death to be on his hands. Back in the early 1860s this was, some thirty or so years back, Fort Zarah or Fort Larned.' He lit a cigarette. 'Reckon that wolf could come through the wall?'

'Only if it's dead.'

'Useful, this pane being gone,' Denton said. 'Got a good sightline and a clear shot. Maybe they knocked it through on purpose. Might've been that fellow we saw or could've been a trapper or some woodsman out there looking for a kip joint. Might even have been one of Borla's rovers. Anyhow — there's no harm in sitting up for the wolf and we may as well see if our other visitor shows up.'

There was a static quality to the snow-compact ground and the air above it was held in complete stillness and it felt as if that ground and woods were listening to a deeper, soundless time. Suddenly, our focus thickened with premonition and into this concentrated sphere of barn light came a figure, moving like a drunk through the drifts, fumbling toward the barn door where it paused, struggling with the latch.

Denton got up, relit the oil lamp, took a hold of his rifle and from the cabin porch called out: 'You, there!'

The figure paused.

Denton raised the oil lamp higher.

The person turned and stalled again and then struggled toward the hut.

As he came closer, Denton said: 'Want to come in?'

But the man stood without moving as new-falling snow settled on his clothes and beard.

'Well, friend,' Denton said, 'it's not much use to either of us to hang around in our frozen bones. Come in and warm up.' Without pausing for dissent, he trudged the few paces back to the cabin door and then turned, perhaps to see if the man had disappeared. He had not.

'This is the weather to perish in,' Denton observed, pushing the door back hard on its hinges and bolting it behind them both.

The stranger said nothing.

'Coffee?'

'Been here fifteen winters,' said the man, standing motionless in the room, 'and the first one I came was like this. When I heard the wolves howling, I grew a fear in my heart because I knew there were only three bullets left in my gun and I had no supplies to go on.'

There was an inevitable pause.

'Coffee,' Denton said more firmly, more carefully. 'Take a seat.'

The man nodded and pulled up a chair. As he heated up the coffee pot, I saw Denton still kept his rifle close. He sat down to roll them each a cigarette and all the while, I surveyed our stranger. Must have been living off the land for some time: was sore-gaunt and rough with solitude. He wore a scarf wrapped closely around his head under a weather-worn hat. His skin looked tanned with filth and he had a beard that climbed right up his cheeks and covered the lower part of his face with mustaches that obscured his mouth and a chin beard that was long and straggle-wild and covered his chest and upper stomach. He spread out both hands on the table, flexing cold-red fingers and I saw they were cut and -

filthy also. He was a being with hunger-salted eyes who carried the look of famish on him. I'd seen such eyes before, in the face of my own strange studio visitor.

When the coffee came, it was good and strong.

'This here, your place?' Denton asked presently.

The man eyed him and cleared his throat. 'When it's empty.'

'What is it to you when the shepherds come down, the ganaderos?'

'Intrusion,' said the man simply. His gaze wandered over Denton's kit. 'You a rancher?'

'Come down on commission. Been called down to catch a wolf. I'm a hunter sometimes, sometimes a painter.'

'What do you paint?'

'What I catch. You hungry?'

The man nodded.

'Beans and bread do you? A little bacon?'

'Do me just right.'

When it was served, I saw the man ate with his fingers, scratching up the hot mess of beans on his bread. He gripped that bit of bread with both hands, glancing up briefly almost as much as blinking, so that the whites of his eyes glimmered and I found them disconcerting.

Denton dished more beans onto the stranger's plate: 'Tell me about yourself. You have a name? Mine's Denton, Jack Denton.'

The man hesitated. 'Bob McGee,' he said.

'Pleased to meet you, Bob.'

'Likewise. I kip here, when I'm not elsewhere. No-one knows,' he muttered and scratched his neck.

'Can't help but see that you're clean worn out. What age do you have on you, if you don't mind me asking?'

McGee paused. 'Depends how old I was in the beginning.'

'Your parents can't tell you?'

'Dead.'

'Both of them?'

McGee said nothing.

'Where'd you sleep?' Denton asked, lighting a cigarette.

'Mostly out in the barn.'

'That'll not do,' said Denton, pulling a fragment of tobacco from his lip. 'You come on in here. Bring a couple of bales with you and you can take your coat off and lay out flat on that.'

McGee gazed steadily at him. 'I'd be obliged,' he said.

Denton rose and cleared off the table and they went out and pulled a hay bale back across the snow and then another and put the moldering stacks in front of the stove.

'I've got a wolfskin you can lie on and another one can go over you.'

'Never slept between wolves before,' McGee said.

'That so? Borla not sling them up by the dozen along these here eaves?' Denton dropped the skins on a bale. 'Well now,' he said, 'it's been a long day and I've gotta get some sleep.'

'I see spirits,' McGee said, his pale eyes half-spun with tears.

Denton paused then.

'Been out here so long, there's more spirits than anything else. Thought you was one.'

XXIII

SÉANCE: E.E. HENRY PHOTOGRAPHIC STUDIO, LEAVENWORTH

Familiar spirit: Jack Denton

IN THE MORNING THE HUT stood deserted because a nest of mangled straw had lain in a corner soaked with urine 'and a night filled with bad dreaming set me up early to find he was gone,' said Denton, passing me as he returned from chucking the wet hay-pile out onto the stoop, now deciding to draw the latchstring through the hut door and there-and-then resolving: 'To keep my pistol on me when awake and by me when asleep,' he said, as he now nailed the window fast where he'd first seen the frame disturbed: 'Should've done that earlier on,' he added and stumped out to feed the horse.

Light prints in the snow crossed from the house to the unbolted barn door and they were fresh on the ground. Denton followed them, cocking his pistol and pushed the outbuilding door ajar with his foot. Inside, the mare stamped and snorted as he went over the place, finding nothing. Then he quieted her, patting her down, until something like silence was held in the dim.

McGee's voice made me start.

'Want me to come out with you today? I know the lie of the land.'

'Whoa,' Denton said to the mare, 'steady now.' He brushed her down as she took her feed. 'Let me think on it,' he said, 'don't want to wear her out.'

There was a pause filled with the horse's champing.

'I've seen them,' said McGee, moving closer into the stall.

'Been watching them. It's her young she runs with. They don't leave her side like normal pups, but go on to live with her. Must be thirty or forty of them all living in a big den. When they hunt, they hunt together.'

'That so,' said Denton, raising the horse's feed bag.

McGee watched him: 'Got any coffee on?'

'Go get it,' said Denton, without turning to look at him. 'It's brewed and waiting. I'll finish up here.' He worked over the mare's flank with a curry comb as McGee trudged toward the hut, shoulders hunched.

'What do you make of him?' said Denton to me, lifting the horse's hind leg. He took a pick to the hoof. 'I'm none too sure myself. We'll see how it goes. God forsakes none, but he's emaciated. At least he'll be a light load for you, Lally,' he said to the mare and stood up, wiping his brow with his arm. 'Wonder if Borla knows about him.

The cabin was strong with coffee fumes when Denton stamped back in. He shook off his coat in a flurry of droplets, laid down his hat and looked at McGee. 'All right,' he said. 'This morning we'll prep the baits and then ride out come noon. Suit you?'

'Suits me.'

'That box there,' Denton pointed, 'and the bottle set and knives. Careful now round those poison bottles. There was a hand out here got his medicine confused with a strychnine phial, they tell me. That's a bad way to go.'

'Not the worst,' said McGee and his voice was distant, full of air.

'Well, Kit — the ranch hand here — had deep gashes to his arms and hands, lips near chewed off and a lacerated tongue.

Takes about three minutes to die and those are the longest three minutes of your life.'

Denton got together ceramic dishes and a strop with the knives, laid out water and cheese. Then he hauled in the frozen side of beef from the outhouse and shaved flesh from its flanks and mixed the cheese and meat substance over heat and chopped and divided it and stuffed it with toxins and then resealed those strychnine-laced, raw beef patties, all the while wearing a pair of blood-soaked gloves. He placed the baits one by one in an open saddlebag and then bridled up the horse and they mounted up and set off when the sun was as bright as it could get on that high-illuminate early afternoon with a light wind that set the trees a-tremor and which bruised my thoughts with cold and they went the full circuit round, but in reverse, and every quarter mile dropped a bait in the snowy grasses, onto dead-cold soil, near a small quarry of rocks, on top of a snow-lined butte and each deposit was also marked with the disguising stench of a skunk skin dragged in the dirt to hide any trace of human touch. Still, no wolves were to be seen but the men paused near some delicate prints scattered in motion on an arroyo track and Denton bent in the saddle to photograph a clear and large paw print: 'That's a significant beast,' he said, returning the camera to its saddle bag. 'Though I'll warrant it's a female one.'

And they returned as the sun-scalded land turned red with snow-patches mottled like poppy blood. They walked the horse back along rough avenues of snow-damaged pines where the path was part-grit and part-ice and the grasses were fused with frost that had not budged in those hours of pallid daylight. Crows swabbed the skyline, their calls subdued and raw, and the desert rock wore its mantle of snow like a shawl. They reached the woods that sheltered the hut at about four o'clock and Denton saw to the horse while McGee raked out the stove and relit it and put the coffee on and a pot of beans and by quarter to five they were plated up and low on talk until replete and then McGee took to his pallet while Denton made the day's journal entry, now quiet, now discrete:

Tuesday January 19th, 1890 — I suggested we take an alternate route round the six mile Grande area to the one I'd already done, this time counter-clockwise and that we lay down strychnine-laced beef which I dropped every quarter-mile or so from my saddle-pack. McGee's now getting used to not touching any of the pre-prepared stuff, leaving me to my hide gloves. He carries a nonplussed air about him at times: blankly reticent. I am doubly aware of his head wound when we are out and his thin, lithe, skeletal arms lightly grip my middle as we plough on through the dirt and snow vista. At times, it feels a little like being gripped by death itself when I can feel his keen bones within his sinuous wrists, when he speaks in that soft, grit-raddled voice in my ear and I am keen to feed him up so that on one side I have the wolf to kill and on the other, the man to heal. Still, I feel all things are sent to us. All things have their wary counterweight.

Found he was riding along with an open knife in his pocket today, point-down like a dagger. Never carry your blade in your pocket like that, I said to him. If it hits your femoral artery, you'll bleed out in under two minutes and there's nothing anyone can do for that. You can't staunch it and you can't seal it up. The blood's eager to get out. He looked mollified and got the blade out. Don't you have some sort of sheath for it, I asked him. I'm going to have to sort him out.

I've set up a small dark room in the outhouse, planking up the window spaces, turning rough and rotted boards into a makeshift bench and there I'll develop my pictures, starting with this one: the paw print. I chucked down one glove on a string next to it — a glove suffused in heifer's blood - and from it I'll gauge the scale though by the looks of it she's got about a 3 1/4" maybe 4" tread there and that'll mean roughly twenty pounds of weight in each inch, making her about an eighty pound animal, maybe slightly less. She's light, all right and probably swift with it — that being a lightweight's advantage, of course. Tomorrow we can get out and check over the baits, see if anything was picked up.

XXIV

SÉANCE: E.E. HENRY PHOTOGRAPHIC STUDIO, LEAVENWORTH

Familiar spirit: Jack Denton

<u>WEDNESDAY JANUARY 20TH, 1890</u> — I am salvaging an old wolf-worry from the back of my brain, coaxed on by this strange hobo-lobo who half-haunts, half-inhabits this disused shepherd hut. We make a strange pair. I look into his keen and brittle eyes and find myself at times more intrigued by this person than by the wolf and her club because he disturbs me somewhat, with his erratic ways. Take the barn, for example, where he can sleep when not persuaded to come in by the stove (though this can have its merits as and when I need to work.) And it is across these initial hunting days he leads me — or seems to lead me, unsure as I am of the accuracy of his know-how. We've been out each morning since Tuesday, seeking the phantom's den and I am not sure who is now leading who on this merry dance. He seemed so sure where to find it. What is certain is the need for another horse or mule, even and I was sore relieved when we returned at noon to find a young heifer and horse tied up in the barn with a note from Borla wishing me well.

When McGee said they are all her pups, the pack, I envisaged some hydra grown in the tundra grasses that blows about like fanged tumbleweed and hunts as a conglomerate mass. If [when] Borla comes down again I will ask him if the phantom's pack is her own offspring. The yellow and the black and presumably others, like her own coat, colored-up like smoke. Do they know? I wonder, as the shadows grow longer in my now-tired will. Do they know we are almost upon them: will change their lives in among the vetch and prairie wild grass, that the stranger now with me has watched them enough to guide us in to them. . .

How much wilder these south woods roar, for a north wind is now among them. The moon this morning was cold and silver like a mercury wound but when the dawn came, the new sun scraped the sky, grazing it to a hard and flushed red. The ground was hard and the air completely clean. We must have looked somewhat medieval with our bobbing lantern that put me in mind of Saint Hubertus and the light hung in the antlers of the stag he hunted. We went slowly. For a while, bar the birds, nothing much stirred. I have filled a page with their silver-gray formations and intend to shoot some down for closer observation.

Not much came of the baits this time but I told McGee not to be too concerned, that it sometimes took a fellow several attempts and that if the wolves had out-wiled my basic approach: meat slit open and injected with poison, I would have to reckon on a more advanced method. Still, today caught us two of her band: the poison baits were dragged off in the grass and I found the carcass of one, small male wolf who should lessen the load. Most of the afternoon was taken up with sketching, once we'd located what was left of the other baits. One was dragged a little ways off and tampered with, another two likewise, one disappeared altogether, the other was untouched and the last had a defiant mound of scat on top as if to show utter contempt. Disheartened, I scooped those baits up and tomorrow will resort to the Newhouse traps. Then we took the carcasses home and skinned them across the afternoon. Will put out more baits tomorrow.

When his black ink ran out and the nib sputtered, Denton refilled his pen with a reddish gall ink and the blotter looked soaked in blood and the scrawl in his journal also looked bloody in its sanguinary lettering. He made character sketches of the man with the damaged head, the cabin air criss-crossed by the sound of his pen:

McGee asked me about the traps and I told him how sometimes a critter will go so far as to chew right through a limb to get away — mostly the smaller ones do that, the foxes, martins, racoons and so on — they'll gnaw right through the bone to get out of their predicament. True, if they're caught in the cold you can hope that the limb is numbed, but it shows you how dire a thing a trap is. These wolf traps have a forty pound drag with them. Slows the animal down and wears it out and it'll get caught, I explained to him, in bushes or rocks. On a riverbed, an animal can drown. The wolf trap has a spread draw of 6 1/2 " and you can use it to catch mountain lions also. Its spread is 8 " and the whole thing with the drag, chain, snap and steel swivel comes in at about 9 pounds. See, what I do is attach extra weight to that device. I attach a log to it, for example, of say 30 pounds and then you have a real problem for the wolf. That'll really wear the animal out as well, lessen its energies when it comes to the slaughtering.

'How many've you got in your time?'

Denton continued his mark-making a moment longer and the nib sounded hard in the fire-lit air. 'It's hard to recall each one and so,' he said, turning to the back of his journal, 'I keep a record. Six hundred and sixty-six exactly.'

There was a long pause as fire-shadow flickered between them.

'You believe she's unnatural?'

'El Fantasma?' Denton took up a brush and wash, applying it to his compressed palette box of pigments. He traced the spine of a sleeping wolf in jaundiced yellow in a workbook. 'What is supernatural occurs between us,' he said, 'between the image and the belief.'

'How so?'

'Like a kind of hallucinated mirage.'

'But a mirage holds a real thing; a ship, or a dog.'

'Yes, but so does the mirage of a wolf. It's thrown out from or onto a real wolf. Or we cast our own fear onto it and so create the very monster we're afraid of.'

'Those Navajo don't think so. Why go to all the trouble of making a conjuration? Just go straight to it. Much easier. Then a werewolf does exist.'

'*Belief* in a werewolf does exist.'

'Much the same thing.'

'Yes, perhaps, to think and to have it so. Then we create them.'

'Then we kill them.'

'It is by contrast that we find ourselves. But what is like, draws like.'

'Those Navajo think it ain't always a wolf, but a witch. Got a special name for it.'

Denton's brush slowed in his hand. 'That's a strong and unusual understanding you hold there.'

'Strong as common in these parts.'

The blue wash of paint glowed in its water across the dusk depiction, before settling into faded aridity as if the watercolor paper were recent rainfall, freshly subsumed by thirsty land. 'I do not have many places left within myself to haunt,' said Denton quietly and washed light again across the page. He stood the workbook on end to dry, propped open and wrote for a long time in his journal again:

Today, on our return, we came upon a cave full of bones like nothing I have ever seen. The cavern seemed to hold the remains of coyote, jackrabbit and deer bones. McGee balked in the first moments, thinking they were human, (he told me later) which was curious to me, when so obviously it was an animal lair, but I do think we might have come across what was once her den. There were clear over a thousand specimens, though it was too dark to see much more — only one hole in the cavern ceiling let through a little extra light — we will have to come back with kerosene lamps tomorrow if we want to investigate more. But I think the den is disused. There were no fresh droppings and the bones were all stripped, dried and old, though the smell in the place is still quite strong. I wonder if there are more dens like this in use along the canyon periphery. This find has given me hope. McGee says he thinks this is the den he first came across a few winters ago, but it was still in use then.

We returned home to skin the baited wolf carcasses and had a good dinner of roast jackrabbit and beans and I finished my painting of the plover while McGee told me a little more of himself. Seems he was doing the shows in Topeka as a curio. He showed me his head and I thought it badly damaged and some of the stitching recent. He keeps vials of morphine with him for when the pain gets bad. Also, he said he was examined once. I asked him what caused the damage and he seemed confused, said something about an attack when he was much younger, a child, but that he gets what he calls his 'frenzied spells' and I couldn't be sure whether the spells were part of the attack or if the attack caused the spells. Apparently, it was out near Fort Larned some thirty or so years ago that this thing took place.

Without looking up, Denton said: 'Okay, let's begin on tomorrow's traps. Stay put, I'll be back in.' Then he closed his journal and with a fresh cigarette stuck in his mouth, pulled on his coat, took an oil lamp, flung open the door and shoved it hard shut behind him. Snow settled in the doorway where he had been.

I got up and followed him.

The barn was cold with a high, dry chill. I could sense the heifer and the horses, but no light in their eyes from the lantern glinted back at me.

Denton had strung up the blood suit in the barn earlier that afternoon. Suspended motionless, it looked like the chrysalis of a hanged man. It cast a long shadow across the hay-strewn floor that traveled along the back of the horse and high up onto the far-timbered wall.

'May as well undress here,' Denton said to himself and stripped. He discarded each garment on a bale of hay. The night was very still, no breeze penetrated the barn cracks, as he sat for a moment, naked and listening. Then he stood up and made for the center of the barn where he tested the ropes and sniffed his blood-dried gloves, lifting them from a hay bale. Silently unknotting the suit, he lowered the bloody costume so that it dangled within his grasp.

Then the first howl came, and it was real close. Denton fumbled for his gun and snuffed out the lantern. He traced the left-hand wall of the barn, peering through its knot holes.

The howl rose again in a cool, clear arc of sound and it scalded my nerves and raised the hair on my body and dried out my mouth.

Denton fitted the rifle muzzle to a small notch in the wood and waited for the wolf to pad into his line of fire, knowing it was after the young heifer. Tense outside sleep, the barn beasts nickered and stamped, yanking at their tether ropes.

'Easy now,' he said to them softly. He crouched on, naked and waiting. Another howl rose, and another resounded. With that, the moon came clear of its patch of cloud and soared into a liquid sky. The notch of wood in which he'd plugged the gun seemed to steady him and in the sudden moonlight, Denton blew the lantern out. 'No light needed now,' he said as the flame died instantly. 'No light but from within,' he murmured, grasping his gun. He eased the barn door open and surveyed the moonlit ground. Nothing. With that came another long, high howl.

My breathing grew fierce, locked to my heartbeat, as Denton maintained a supernatural focus. Then, the wolf came into view and stood watching him. She was lithe and small and intelligent and she was standing in the middle of the barn.

Time burred and thickened between them and in that moment it became clear to me the impossibility of Denton moving his hand toward the gun stock, the impossibility of hooking the trigger with his finger, the sheer impossibility of taking his eyes from her: 'El Fantasma,' he murmured, and then the she-wolf was gone.

XXV

SÉANCE: E.E. HENRY PHOTOGRAPHIC STUDIO,
LEAVENWORTH

Familiar spirit: Jack Denton

NEXT DAY DENTON SLAUGHTERED the heifer, forcing her to kneel before he slit her throat. He hung the dripping, white-eyed carcass upside down, then beheaded it. This was the main bait. He cut up and divided cheese and kidney fat in an enamel basin, stewing them before dividing the substance with a bone knife when it cooled. Then he made a hole in each lump and pushed a capsule of cyanide and strychnine into that hole and then sealed it over again with cheese. He wore his entire blood suit this time and blood-steeped gloves and put the bait into a rawhide bag rubbed over with blood. He stood still for a moment, dressed in dried blood.

Then they went out.

They dragged the circuit with the roped innards of the young cow and left a bait each half mile or so, before reaching a snow-shielded gulley whose overhanging rocks kept the snow-drifts at bay, a bit of ground some six miles off from the cabin. And Denton dismounted and crouched in the dirt and deciphered small signs, shifting his balance and discovered scat mounds and a scattering of rodent bones and looking up saw a large pile of earth near a cleft in the rock. He stood up real slow and made a sign for hush at McGee who neared him, now slowing also. Denton pointed at the den and McGee nodded, understanding him. They worked in quiet syncopation: McGee drew the horses off to a small gulley down-wind and roped them to a pine tree, then Denton lifted a shovel, a sifter and four traps from the travois and motioned for McGee to stay with the horses while he set them.

He went over to the clearing in the boulders, chose a backing of rock and rhythmically cleared the ground of its frozen topsoil with a bone knife. He made a dent in the loosened earth and bedded down the first trap with a cotton square laid on top, set to be sprung with the lightest pressure. Then he firmed up the trap bed, pressing the dirt down hard with both his gloved hands. Meticulously, Denton began to replace the earth in stages and because that earth was snowless, the laying went easier. Using a sifter he scattered soil over the bed that was clear of twigs and grit and pebbles and the cotton protected the space in the trap and he smoothed the area over that trap with a small stick. Then he used the rougher, cleared dirt piled on a bit of burlap to further disguise the whole area, fastidiously smoothing it over with a metal spoon and finally he blended that topsoil in with leafy debris and small stones. Then he spaded out dirt to make a hole against the rock backing and in it he placed the bait. It was now noon. By two, the remaining contaminated baits were laid near another three traps and the heifer's head was laced with poison.

McGee stood, patiently watching over the horses as Denton tramped back over to him, panting in short cloud-breaths and yanked off his cowhide gloves.

'We should head back,' he said, taking a long drink from the water flagon. 'Job's done. Isn't any use to sit out here freezing to death waiting on them.'

But McGee suddenly pointed then, as a small shape rounded the rock point and they stood still, unspeaking. The wolf mounted the red-stone summit and surveyed them for a long moment. Denton reached for the saddle holster and fired at her, but she slipped back down the escarpment and trotted down the trailhead to vanish among an old stand of piñons.

'Damn,' said Denton. 'She's onto us.'

Then they drew out of that gulley as the light dipped and set off for the cabin again. Denton stripped in the barn, then loosened the girths on the horses and removed their bridles and gave them water and brushed them down, shouting to McGee who lugged the kit into the hut: 'Heat up some water — I'm sickened by blood — and bring me a blanket, I'm nearly done.'

And he strung up the blood suit and wrapped himself up in Mexican wool and padded nakedly across the frozen ground. When he re-entered the steamy cabin, the tin bath was filled with stove-melted snow and lowering himself into hot water, Denton took some lye and a scrubbing brush and gave himself a good going over, singing as he washed himself down. Suds soaked the floor in a brownish tidemark and when Denton stood up, those same suds were brackish with blood. He got into fresh clothes and threw the old water on the snow outside, brewed up a coffee pot and started writing up the day's notes as all the while McGee rocked in the rocker, looking at prints in the faded Spanish bible and hummed softly to himself.

Friday January 22nd, 1890 — All is well in the wolving world though it was hard going today. We made a rough travois from pine strips and loaded up the ten Newhousers and chains onto it. Four of those traps I prepared with a goose feather dipped in bear oil and attached to those were my customized drags, anchor-like shapes, that will catch in the arroyo rocks and branches and pull at wolf flesh, to slow the caught animal right down.

Going not so tough at first: slush in the woods, but then the ground was drier toward the canyon and the travois got stuck every few feet in the rocks so that I let McGee lead while I jumped down and walked alongside to keep freeing it. But we were rewarded: we finally found the den some six miles out, coming across it quite by accident. It is an enclave scooped out of the red canyon rock disguised by a small butte of fine sandstone. And at last I've seen El Fantasma in daylight and she is a resplendent Mexican wolf with a sandy, yellowish-gray pelage. Beige hues and a gold-yellow color decorate her skull fur and the nape of her neck. She has a blackish collar of fur and a hide that varies between sandy-gray and cream, highlighted in tawny browns, whites and blacks so that the effect when she runs is indeed of rippling smoke. I have seldom seen so compact and perfect a specimen. She is small, but evidently very strong and robustly keeps charge of her grown and half-grown whelps as they gambol in the snowy places. I felt a strange heart joy - an elation to find this terrain, so soon to become a killing field. I also feel we might rest for a while. If she has picked up our scent, she will be on the alert and we must lull her into a false sense of security again.

It took us nearly three hours to do the rounds and then the four traps were tough to set, the ground being so hard. We came back stiff and saddle sore and in need of a drink, but McGee refused it. I had a good, hot soak and will paint a couple of birds I've shot. McGee's bunked down early, being careful how he lays down his head.

I've thought more on this strange, damaged man. He reminds me of what the Arikara call the 'Scalped Man'. He is the one who can't return to his tribe once so damaged and exists — a kind of living ghost — in a cave or some other dwelling, outside of society, of family, of kinship. Do the ganaderos know much of his existence? I doubt it. I see cunning etched into his features, the way other men possess laughter lines. Anyhow, it seems McGee was telling me the truth when he spoke about what happened to him. There was even a petition to Congress made some time ago. Now he wants to make another one. I have the medical letter he showed me, by way of anatomical examination, which I'll copy out while he's sleeping:

Dear Sir,

I am an old man now and doubtless this will be the last case I shall examine. You are aware of Robertson's article: *Remarks on the Management of the Scalped Head* and as such, know of the bore hole techniques described therein. The flesh will swell often beyond the skull and within the bore holes and any necrotic (that is to say blackened) flakes should be removed by means of an awl. It will escape no-one's sense of irony that those flakes are described as being somewhat the size of a dollar.

I have made an advancement on such procedures through direct examination of a unique example of so-called scalping or evulsion of the scalp. In this case — the case of Robert McGee — healing has commenced through secondary intention, though the suture lines are relatively fresh.

The specimen is roughly thirty-four years old and brings with him a show card detailing the rather lurid facts surrounding the case. Be they fact or fiction, I am also to inform you that he has been subjected to three other wounds inflicted to the area in question, namely a blow from a dull object or knife, possible damage from an encounter with a wild animal or brawl and further tearing to the dermis from sporadic seizures which the subject suffers from.

I am given to believe his first surgery was in 1864 at a field hospital in Kansas under the care of Surgeon Hulbert H. Clarke. Subsequent treatments have been variable and sporadic. It goes without saying that Reverdin's groundbreaking research in the field had not yet seen the light of day in 1864 Kansas, even if the events were postdated to 1869. Without a doubt, something of a surgical phenomenon presents itself in the intricate overlay of medical material, in this anatomy of a scalping.

However, equal consideration must be given to the assertion that the subject said he 'suffered fits' and was being prescribed bromide salts as an hysterical epileptic. Potassium bromide may have induced a number of contraindications affecting the central nervous system. Present would be lethargy, severe skin reactions, physical wasting, cachexia, paresis, delirium and psychosis.

Let me put a colleague's unusual supposition to you as follows: from what we can gather, we have a supplies train crossing country known to be challenging. Their escort has left them, or they had none in the first place, and they are tired. It is extremely hot. In general they are anxious, sometimes frightened by small things — an unusual movement of bird flocks, for example, or a sinister-seeming stillness. One day, the overall fear of the party reaches fever pitch. The heat is excessive. Riders are seen at the herd, but nothing happens. Then, when a drover's gun misfires, the signal is made. What ensues is collective hysteria, a psychic attack. The whole wagon train's foreboding is so great as to manifest a vision of violence. They may all have suffered a massive psychological disturbance, driven by the dread of what might happen. Unusual things come from unexpected places, my colleague argues, the body being a stranger magnifier than we sometimes suppose.

However, I consider this far-fetched in the extreme and prefer to assume that in McGee's case, due to medicines he may have been prescribed, his epilepsy was heightened by the bromides and arguably, he hallucinated a physical, psychosomatic reaction much stronger than the reaction of those with him. Added to this, it is also highly possible that he suffered a seizure and independently damaged his cranium and cranial dermis in a fall sustained during the attack which may not have been inflicted by anything but circumstance. It is likely, as in such unusual cases, that we will never ascertain a proper understanding of events, but I am confident his physiognomy will warrant further examinations.

Dr. McAlister,
Washington D.C. 1888

I have known bobcats with peculiarly human looking faces and they behave with the exact same fear as us when confronted with their imminent death. Today, squinting at the wolf we are hunting, I found myself recognizing a most disconcerting thing. To me, McGee possesses that same scrutinizing stare. It is as if he has not become an underdog but an underwolf, and I wonder how he came to be out here for quite so long. How did he survive? I asked him, in those intervening years.

He gave me a creased advertisement for a dime hall entertainment, and it was strange to see his name in print:

EDEN MUSEE,

Week Commencing March 14.

Mr. Robert McGee,
The Scalped Man.

The Famous Rinehart Family.

MISS DOLLIE WILLIAMS,
The Musical Queen.

10 C - ADMITS TO ALL - **10** C

I heard from a rancher that they are planning to raze this hut come the spring as it is so run-down and wonder where he would be then, if that is the case. So, I've resolved to help him. Seems only fair that he should benefit from this kill after the companionship and help he's given me. Surely bounty money will set him to rights. Says he's going to pick up with the sideshows again: has some fantasy about touring Scotland with that Wild West Show. Try to find some roots, he says. Well, roots cost money and on we must go. The smoke-wolf must die tomorrow, though my heart is already conflicted. It is merely tiredness, I suspect. If she's refused the trap, I will try the bait again and failing that, will dig a pit. Seems to me, there are many ways to catch a wolf.

XXVI

SÉANCE: E.E. HENRY PHOTOGRAPHIC STUDIO,
LEAVENWORTH

Familiar spirit: Jack Denton

TWO DAYS LATER THEY were mounted up and set out again. Denton rode with his hat brim pulled right down and leaned back in the saddle a little so as to survey the land. The tundra lay still, frosted and magnificent, and the wind was down a little. Nothing much moved. Only sunlight cropped the bruised shadow-line of pines, where small streams buried deep in banks of snow. Then they reached the place.

Had it not been for the fear in her eyes and the blood-tinged stain seeping from her leg where the metal teeth of the trap caught her hard, it might have been the she-wolf herself that lay in wait for the men, as they walked the horses down the steep gully bank. Every slight shuffle and soft growl was nicked with a spasm of pain.

'Looks like she's been at the bait,' said Denton as he dismounted. He passed the reins to McGee and went over to where the wolf crouched, nudging the meat with his boot. Then he took both horses a little way off, tied them securely to one another and fastened them to a tree. They stamped and whinnied as the wolf gave a high and protracted howl. Hobbling, she turned within the limits of the trap, returning to the self-same position in which she was caught.

'Foot's near come off,' said McGee, standing a little ways off.

'Careful,' Denton cautioned and trudged over slowly.

'She's a fierce one.'

'What did you expect?' He lit a cigarette and stood with one foot raised on a rock, surveying the bloody wolf.

'Thought she might be dead.'

The she-wolf growled, and pulled at the trap.

'Easy now,' Denton said.

'How's she caught? Is she free? I can't see her held.'

'She's going nowhere with that drag. We better take care of her before she makes a run for it again. She's caught good for now, but you never know.'

'You after shooting her?'

'Don't want to ruin the pelt. We're going to rope her. Done anything like that before?'

McGee shook his head.

'Stay here.' Denton returned to the tethered horses and untied two lariats attached to the saddle horn on the mare and walked back to the wolf. 'Watch,' he said. He swirled the first rope high above his head and the wolf watched him, unblinking. He got a good momentum going, and then flung it with a strong clear aim. The lasso landed with a burring sound around the wolf's neck.

'Number two,' said Denton and did it again. The she-wolf lashed out, cowering and snarling with fear, but he stood firm, a rope in each hand, and each hand clad in a heavy rawhide glove. 'Get over here and give me your gloved hand.'

McGee held out his hand, palm upward, fingers together and Denton walked behind him, lifting one of the ropes up and over his head.

'You're a left-hander?'

McGee nodded.

Denton gave him an end to grasp with a further length swinging loose and then wrapped the rope as if already winding in the wolf, across and around McGee's palm repeatedly.

'Stay there,' he said. 'Stand firm, now, legs apart. She'll go hard, if she goes, and I need you to hold her firm until we can mount up.' He moved away from McGee, coiling the second rope end around his arm. 'I'm going to walk you to the horses,' he said.

They went like early circle-makers whose central pin was a trapped beast, but the circuit they made was rough and imperfect. I watched as every so often the wolf pulled at them, hard.

'We have to move swiftly now,' Denton said. 'You get on up there and ride this horse a little way over there to that rock.' He pointed. 'I'm going over there, beyond the wolf. When I make the sign of the cross, I want you to kick in and spur your horse on in a straight trot, right over to that large outcrop. Understood? Try and make it a swift start, even if you have to slow her up afterward. We have to go quick and quiet now.'

McGee did as he was instructed, mounted up and moved off to the small rock. Mounting his own horse, Denton walked the mare in a wide arc around the wolf to the north of the gulley. The piebald reared once, as the tang of wolf reached her nostrils. He held her to a walk and then, when he was out beyond the trapped wolf, made the horse stand as he turned in the saddle.

I took it all in, saw the she-wolf rise, her rear leg cramped in pain, saw her cower and snarl in the snowy light.

Denton reached in his saddlebag, got out a camera and swiftly took her photograph.

Then he gave the sign.

Whether it was fluke or nerves, both men kicked off hard and the wolf only struggled for a few moments until blood burst from her mouth.

IT IS always the same: the drop from terror reducing magnificence to dumbness. The trap made this its glyph and sharp on the trap's jaws followed the rope and the rope deadened the living in a long instant, not making the wolf fall from life, but fall into death. It carried silence in its twine and numbness in its contact. Death: the underwhelmer. It was done.

'Yet I would've felt the strain of that rope in my palm burn for the rest of my life,' said Denton to me, pausing awhile to catch his breath. 'As if branded with a reading that described not a huntsman, but a killer.'

They cleaned up. Seemed almost too easy to spring the traps and gather them up, unhitch the fetid calf head from its bait hook, pull apart the trap jaws from the she-wolf's blood-ragged hind leg. Sticky musculature showed frayed to the bone from the struggle. They bound her up with the same ropes they'd throttled her with, raised her bladder-seeping carcass onto the back of the mare who scuffed the ground and jerked with fear. Then they mounted up and rode with the stiffening body in its ropes across terrain that recalled the recent spring of her pads and the weight of her belly rolled in freshly fallen snow. They rode on some four miles in the mounting silence of noon, broken only by crow calls.

Two miles from the log hut, Denton pulled up and let the wolf down, heavy with death. They undid her tethers, reworking the knots into a rough harness. Then they tied the length of the ropes to Denton's worn saddle pommel and set off again, hunched on their horses with the she-wolf's body like a sled, running the snow as a scent-drag behind them. Her death trail lay deep across those mesa drifts.

'Snow'll preserve the scent,' Denton called to McGee, 'it'll hold her blood smell for longer. Scare any others off.'

It was a frozen corpse they hauled into the barn come late noon, undoing the tight cords. She lay stiffly on the damp straw, as if still bound, and they stood back awhile, gazing at her. Denton smoked and McGee smoked and they just stood looking at her. The horses nickered once in a while as scent from the body lifted on the breeze. The wolf seemed a pale grayish color now, as if blood had drained from her nervous system, drained from her fur tips, as if receding blood had caused her hide to whiten. Now she lay a base, creamy gray and her snout, though black, took on that gray and her eyes seemed a gelled gray: a glutinous mass of burst sight.

There was a smell of shame about the barn, I felt.

McGee turned and made for the hut as Denton dropped his cigarette stub and its smoke dwindled in the moist straw before he crushed it under the heel of his boot. 'This is science,' he said to himself. 'A means to an end. A science.' And with that he flicked open a pocket-knife and knelt and stabbed at the wolf's lower gut and then in a rough, sawing motion, slit her belly open. There, in a shining wrap, were wolf fetuses like pale seeds in a soft, red fruit. Denton scooped them out as he sang softly to himself a verse from the old, lupine love song:

> Wolf I'll have thee in my palm,
> obey me girl, the day is done.
> Pups are hidden in thy belly,
> I'll see to them when I destroy thee.

'And there'll be a yellow moon,' he sang, cupping the wolf whelps in his hand as he made his way back to the cabin, 'shining softly, all alone.'

II

The Carte de Visite

I

WILD WEST PHOTOGRAPH
LEAVENWORTH, 1890

ROBERT MCGEE'S DAMAGED SCALP was to me a mangled flag of stars and stripes. Boots, a fire rake, wagon awnings, sawdust, oil lamps, grasses. He manifested them all in his stitched-up cranium. Knocked unconscious, the stars had flashed, revealing a set of torn-up stripes. In fleshy striations, those blue days burned. And so, positioned and arranged in three-quarter profile, I knew by instinct not to picture him head on. Not to engage his stare. Not to show the other scars. To only display the head wound, the delicate cicatrix, after carefully unwinding his newspaper skull-cloth. A plain background would be required. No ferns or plants of any kind. No globes or plinths. No gesture of revelation on the victim's part. No focus on the wound itself, just the normalcy of the workaday man who sat before me must be taken in, ingested with curious sympathy by those who then saw him. They must not be revulsed or shocked. Must not be angered or reduced to tears. Must be made to feel that he was one of them and that the fabric of his being was born under the same banner as theirs, though his image was now a frontispiece to an otherwise everyday experience, though his own book of days now contained this pressed American flag — faded and stained and recalcitrant — between its battered pages.

And so, like a barber-surgeon, I moved around my sitter, touching him lightly with deft fingers that carefully negotiated a neckerchief, assessed a rough collar. McGee sat quite still as I tended him, like an ancient priest preparing the statue of a deity in order that its rangy spirit could re-enter the wood or gold, plaster or stone, could seep into his bashed-in musculature and skin, could ripple through the deteriorated contours of his pate, could enliven and lift his damaged limbs. Of which deity that spirit was, I couldn't say: I doubt it was his earlier, orphaned, protesting god, I doubt it was the god of the spirit of America (if such a thing exists), I doubt it was the death spirit which had glanced off him in the high grasses, I doubt it was the spirit of violence — he so mild now, so terminally broken — except that perhaps an in-soaked resistance came to wash through his veins, something like the resistance of those sun-beaten '64 plains, but I found his resignedness an irritant and resolved to inject him with a fresh spirit of revenge.

Everything was in its place. I positioned him where the bruising wouldn't show in the final paper imprint, having painted arnica onto his cheekbone and anointed his other cuts and scrapes with alcohol and antiseptic. I felt his damage rested heavily on me: his resolved waiting, his patience, his presence, matched the weight of his wounds. Felt those blue eyes dart over me when I moved away to fetch a bottle, adjust a level, draw a blind. And when I returned, I felt those eyes avoid me again, now fixed on a red dot painted on the opposite wall, dabbed on for the illusion of focus, (though many who came to the studio were trained in the sightline of the gun, could fire an accurate shot like accurately pouring a drink. Simple, quiet, swift.)

Then, cloaked in the camouflage of the photographer's mantle, I summoned his image into being and the morning light held still for me, as if complicit. In silver salts and glass, evident spirits devoured the moment — mine was the visionary tent in a high, quivering, American mirage. As I worked, the studio hung heavy in a premonition of simple capture, silence rising like heat. And in doing all this, I slowly acknowledged a growing repulsion toward my sitter.

It wasn't the rank layers of filthy clothing arranged on his unwashed and injured body (I thought the smell and hurt would pervade his portrait — give the pose a certain grit.) It was not the intensity of his gaze that followed the contours of my own form in its neat, hand-sewn waistcoat of calico stars stitched in navy and dun: as if gauging how a man's body in health should move. It was not the strange rasp in his voice which seemed to catch in badly held emotion. It was simply that I sensed him as a half-being: that his spirit now moved between worlds and forms, shifting in and out of his tattered pelt, that he was a man whose existence lay between. Fact was, he had no true existence. Fact was, he was alarming in that. Fact was, no employer would have properly considered him; none who had a modicum of understanding around how it was that his reality worked. Life has no energy for broken spirits. They wash in and out of their own accord.

I lifted the glass from the camera frame as the first one was done: 'Have you the slide of the wolf?' He retrieved it from his pocket lining, held the box a little too long in the touch of our transaction.

I left him sitting there for a moment to examine them. I had two negatives now: one of the subject — so detailed, so finely caught — and the collected-up slide of El Fantasma, the smoke wolf. I had captured them both. I slotted the wolf into the wooden-framed spirit box, then McGee's own portrait, then the light-sensitive paper and the man and the wolf came together in the amber glow of the studio safelight. It was done. This was not McGee's ticket to the show-world, but a token for my father. 'Now he will yield,' I said to myself, in my own mind believing ghosts procured love.

YOU WILL not believe me when I say I did not know Robert McGee was the wolf-hunter's companion. That his rough bearing and strange manner and intensive looks could be mistaken for someone else entirely. I did not even know my sitter's name and thought the man in the vision was the McGee he had summoned without realizing it was a self-summoning. And I wondered how I could see McGee at all, considering he was still alive — how his spirit could operate within the séance whilst also sitting at the table in the studio. How he traversed both worlds. I became a damaged man by thought-walking my visitor's own damaged history. That at his center glowed a bad star. The seed of its intent was malign — a little like the grit in Neighbor's spawning snowflake — and that in my reckoning now, all iterations of that star must so be malign. Malign to the touch, malign to the taste.

What I had experienced was inexplicable, except in visionary form. I went in calm and emerged dazed and in a state of shock. Was it a dream of a prayer? It was like no sitting I'd ever been in. An amalgam of vistas and stenches, dusts and blows, I emerged sun-scorched and bruised. Sometimes saddle-worn, sometimes drunk. I know I went with a woman, one night. I still have the clothes on that were stained by her blood. At all times, it was as if I were there and as if the spirits who came to speak with us knew me, as if they had guided my companion in to the set.

He had sat up very straight, obliging. I was keen to see how it would work and kept the oil wick at a low busk. When the time came, I saw his concentration thicken and he grew pale, eyelids flickering. Beads of sweat streaked his brow when the first voice came through him and it was very high and very faint, like a distant child calling in a strong wind.

Once, within a scene of attack, he began to violently shake and foam at the mouth. When he fell to the floor, I realized he was having a spell and put a wooden ruler between his teeth and held his head still in my lap. It was too late to get Slaine, I thought, as he shuddered for a while and then lay still.

We resumed, though he was paler than ever. I watched his surgery at the fort, ignored the sharp taps at the studio window by those who refused to believe CLOSED FOR THE DAY was certain. A different kind of spirit rapping, those flesh and bone fingers fell silent as disappointed clients turned away in the wind. Money meant nothing to me then: I only needed the vision. Getting up to secure the shutters, I saw the small man of March had fallen: my tin keeper of the cold house of dream.

Time wore on and we crossed the country, stopping for a while in an old bordello. I would have given my all to photograph some of those ephemeral faces: the whores and their clients, tumultuous, tremendous. When we entered snow, wolves came to summon us. There were anatomists, a court case and surgeons. This was his world of corporate fairgrounds: medical, judicial and show-hall. By nightfall, the wolf was dead and a final image cut me to the quick. I saw a man with a camera, photographing her corpse in an arroyo and when he turned to look at me, thought I saw my own face.

At last my querent grew faint and then no other spirit voices came to us. He asked forgiveness. It was given. Asked for blessing. It was granted. And when, like the upraising of some ominous dawn, the lamp flame was finally brought up again, I saw that the stranger had been weeping. Had been down on the knees of his heart. In his own strange circumstance, looked soiled and demolished. Reticence was poised as politeness curbed us and shaken, I poured out a couple of drinks.

"All things exist," I'd said faintly, by way of comfort to the man whose glass glinted, already drained. "All things exist," I'd said, "real or imagined."

I WILL tell you now how the vengeance was and it was this: that McGee used his own image to avenge himself of an attack which he said created the very skin and bone of his depiction. That his photograph retaliated by turning its apparent truth to lies — in turn stripped itself of fallacious meaning, so that its falsehood could shrivel up and decay, so that everything in it which seemed true became untrue, so that clarity damned where subtlety might have saved. . . if only I had chosen a different name, if only I had desisted from naming at all. You cannot convert delusive wisdom, cannot pull back on history's reins. I have no real proof but suspicion and dreams: my sleep is uneasy. The picture turns to a pool of grease and shadow shafts and I wake up broken. Revenge within revenge: I'd tried to create a situation and am now embroiled in the conditions of its making. Look once: you see a scalped man. Look again: a vast wound for a scalping. Look once: a legacy of native violence. Look again: there is no such person as Sioux Chief Little Turtle.

He is my own Wild West invention.

Because I believe invention is better than cure — when prevention has passed — or at least, reinvention. Now, the image reverts. True/false, true/false, flipping in the imagination. I thought: maybe I can repay McGee, counterbalance the raree show and scalpel. His was a lot spent in those weird and unholy theaters. He ranged through them as a spectacle of himself. I thought he could do better. Could maybe raise his game a little; his sights. Anyhow, I cooked up the name and spelt it out so that really it wasn't the photograph after all — the photograph came after the fact (or the fiction, to be accurate and precise in my thinking.) It was a subterfuge and I had written on this carte-de-visite, a brand like one might brand a tin of beans, something to hold the mind, something to sell his face, and the brand was this:

SCALPED BY SIOUX CHIEF LITTLE TURTLE IN 1864

Turtles came to mind as I had a lithograph of one on the studio wall and what with that court case, that Minnesota trial which saw thirty-eight Lakota hanged from the neck in 1862, I thought that tribe still carried some traction out here, though they never were this far south and by 1890, I must tell you, many had died, or been fought off, or put out onto their dusty little parcels of land and left to fend for themselves. And I thought the brand must have the lineaments of high stress: it must carry some volatile weight. No good saying it was a group of starving adolescents as McGee had originally told me it was: we needed some clout and so I made this invented person a Sioux chief. There you have it.

The head wound — who knew? Looked like he'd recently had it opened up again and resealed. The catgut was still visible and it was a fair mess of assorted colors. I wondered if he'd had those dizzy spells from childhood, wondered if he'd perhaps got caught up in something else entirely. Hobos like him get beaten up pretty regularly. Maybe he'd been riding the trains, something like that. He had a small bit of cash for me from the wolf bounty, he said. I declined it as there was more than enough personal compensation for me in that spirit photograph.

'The end of drudge,' as Tudor said, not truly knowing what drudge was. 'Except when I mark their books,' he said, 'sitting up all night with ink stains and arithmetic and wonder what it is we teach them out here, chalked up in resolute fictions.'

WHO WAS this man whose history took so many forms? He seemed vulnerable as a ghost. I took my victim to the showmen and penmen and they assessed him and included him in their annals of pretense, were greedy for elaboration. Go to Cody, go to Inman and McGee leaves powder prints across the broadsheets of their fame. While I gave him a face and an attacker's name, they embellished the concoction and put him on display and all the while I suspect he was receding, receding from the assemblage he had become. He flickered between our living world and the world of the dead. Needed material evidence to prove to himself his own charged and voluble worth.

Robert McGee — like all those pioneering others — had inevitably transgressed, caught in the trail of greed, lies and slaughter. And here he was, a stitched and tattered, flesh and blood, barely living American flag. He was a rag and bone boy, a scarecrow, a tatterdemalion to shoo off the crows of progress, still scavenging on un-promised land. He — like so many — was a pioneer sacrifice. A startling reminder of the price of enforced progress. Less than an image, more than an invention. He was — and still is — only one page, one picture, one fabrication in a battered and battering American book of the dead.

END

The Manifest

E.E. Henry (*photographer*)

The Rev. Henry (*Eben's father*)

Montgomery Slaine (*doctor*)

Tudor Walker (*teacher*)

Robert McGee (*adult: itinerant*)

Allen Edwards (*drover*)

Hulbert H. Clarke (*surgeon*)

J.R.R. Hanna (*nurse*)

Robert McGee (*boy: drover*)

Jerome Crowe (*wagon master*)

Dock Brockman (*herdsman*)

William C. Human (*captain*)

Rebekah Crowe (*Jerome's wife*)

Ruth Crowe (*Jerome's daughter*)

Jack Burd (*interpreter*)

George Bent (*interpreter*)
and Magpie (*George's wife*)

Setangya (*chief*)

James Parmetar (*captain*)

Catalina Alvira Chaireses (*Carlos' sister*) Abraham Tunks (*private*)

Abner Jameson (*private*)   Junius Browne (*embalmer*)

Ned Jones (*private*)   Angelina de las Estano-Estrellas (*prostitute*)

Carlos de Lopez (*salon owner*)

Nathaniel Flint (*Sin Eater*)

Elizabeth Flint de Lopez

Jack Denton (*hunter*)

Frank Borla (*rancher*)

ACKNOWLEDGEMENTS

My deepest gratitude to the Nightwalker: Aaron Kent for his own vision and belief in all things strange; to my literary agent, Nemonie Craven, for her wisdom, acumen and support; to editor Cathleen Allyn Conway (RIP, 1861) for her concision, precision and an eagle eye; to dear Spaniard-in-another-life, Virginia FitzRoy; to the generous and much-admired Cairìne MacGillivray, for vision and notation; and to my beloved Alexis Thompson.

Images of and relating to E.E. Henry and the letter from his father, the Reverend Thomas Henry, are reproduced with kind permission from the Archival Collection at the Ottawa Museum. Portrait of Setangya by William S. Soule, National Anthropological Archives, Smithsonian Institution. The image of Captain C. Human reproduced with kind permission from the Missouri Valley Special Collections, Kansas City Public Library.

LAY OUT YOUR UNREST

www.ingramcontent.com/pod-product-compliance
Ingram Content Group UK Ltd.
Pitfield, Milton Keynes, MK11 3LW, UK
UKHW040102110125
453471UK00004B/45